Praise for Naomi Booth

Animals at Night

'Naomi Booth is a master of the short story, and this collection is stunning.' – **Lucie McKnight Hardy**

Exit Management

'Compelling, formally innovative and beautifully conceived.' – ***The Guardian***

'A bittersweet and truthful portrait of people still finding their places in the world.' – ***i News***

'[A] compelling contemporary read crammed with insight and compassion.' – **Val McDermid**

Sealed

'Gripping... enough to make your skin tingle.' – ***New York Times***

'Marvellous.' – ***The Guardian***

'[A] brilliant dystopian distillation of just about all the ecological fears a young parent can suffer from.' – ***The White Review***

The Lost Art of Sinking

'A short, absorbing read about losing yourself that packs a compelling punch.' – ***Grazia***

'Naomi Booth is a name to watch.' – ***Prospect***

Also by Naomi Booth

Exit Management

Sealed

The Lost Art of Sinking

Animals at Night

dead ink

First published in Great Britain in 2022 by Dead Ink, an imprint of Cinder House Publishing Limited.

Print ISBN 978-1-911585-86-2
Ebook ISBN 978-1-911585-87-9

Editing by Ella Chappell
Proofreading by Dan Coxon / dancoxon.com
Cover design by Luke Bird / lukebird.co.uk
Cover image by Jeff rogues / Getty
Typeset by Laura Jones / lauraflojo.com

Printed and bound in Great Britain by Clays Ltd, Elcograf S.p.A.

www.deadinkbooks.com

Animals at Night

Naomi Booth

dead ink

Contents

For Betty

Strangers

My mother's night-time singing repertoire veered between the sacred and the profane—'Jesus Wants Me for a Sunbeam' segued into 'My Father's a Lavatory Cleaner'. Kneeling next to me in the dark, she smelt of her evening application of Nivea and of the hair lacquer that she brushed out before bed in clouds of perfumed scurf. I slept in the attic of our narrow, terraced house in the room above hers, and the scuffle of mice in the roof often frightened me. When I called for her, my mother would always come. She held my hand, and her voice was thick and glitchy as she sang to me—*Some say that he died of a fever/ Some say that he died of a fright/ But I know what my father died of/ He died of the smell of the—*

♦

Had I *really* thought about it, the registrar asked me yesterday, peering over his glasses. Had I really considered how difficult and—he'd paused for the right words here, for maximum impact—*unpleasant and upsetting* it might be?

I've a tremor in my right eyelid and I haven't been able to sleep properly for the last two nights. But I've done the research. I know that what I'm doing is legit. I stood my ground with the registrar and got all the necessary certificates. Still. My body hasn't got the message. I've got an anxious bladder and I keep stalling the bloody van. Come on, Liz, keep it together. Bradford Royal Infirmary. Here we go. Follow the signs to Cardiology, then take the narrow loop road that's signposted *Staff Only*. I've to keep going down here, that's what the man said, until I reach the sub-station. I pull up on the double-yellows. A white plastic plaque screwed to the redbrick wall up ahead reads, *Boiler House Sub-Station*. There's a large chimney rising behind this building, which makes me think of clinical waste and incineration. Don't think about it. Don't think about it, Liz, or you'll lose your nerve.

I jump down from the van. I knock hard on the metal double-doors. Dead sound. No one will hear. No one will hear and then I'll have to go home and call the whole thing off. And I could do it in good faith: I tried, Mum, I tried. Except, here we go. The doors clatter open.

Liz, is it? a smiling man says to me. Must be the one I spoke to earlier, who told me he'd meet me here where it was quiet to avoid any *fuss*. He has a kindly face. He's in his fifties, perhaps. A man who looks like he's softened with age, like butter left out of the fridge.

She's all ready, he's saying. And I've changed her into the natural cotton... *outfit* for you.

Thank you, I say. That's kind of you. I know this must be... a bit unusual—

No. No. Not at all. I'm pleased you're taking her away. I wish more people would, really.

There's a trolley in the corridor behind him. White shroud. Obscure figure underneath it. Can I really do this? Medicinal smell. Slightly woozy feeling, strange taste on my tongue, like when you spray too much perfume. Can I do it? Yes, yes, I'll have to because now he's wheeling the trolley out, right out the double doors, towards the side of my campervan. And he's picking up the shroud, scooping it up—*her* up. She's collapsible, in his arms. He carries the bundle without reservations or any visible squeamishness.

Her body will be soft again. I've researched all of this too. I've timed it so that the rigor mortis will have passed.

Where do you want her? he says.

There's a roadmap marked with neon Post-Its on the seat next to me, a small bag packed with essentials in the foot well, and all the paperwork is in a file in the glovebox. In my rear-view window, I see the man pulling the metal doors closed behind him. It's really happening then. I'm alone with her.

Settle in, belt up. First stop: the west coast. Mum planned this route for me. For us. She wanted me to take her across to Edna, her oldest friend, then down to see my Grace, her beloved granddaughter. And then we're to end up somewhere near the sea. *What about going down to Patricia?* she'd said. *You could do with seeing Patricia. How long has it been since all of that?* Mum knew how to salt a wound. There was no hiding anything from her for long.

It's been a while since I've driven any real distance in the campervan. It's been sitting on Steve's driveway, though the divorce settlement gave me custody. I check both mirrors again, find that bite point, pull away smoothly. Yes, Liz, nicely done. Except—shit—the first corner, accelerating a little harder than I intend, and there's a nasty thud. She's rolling, hitting against something in the back of the van.

Sorry! I call over my shoulder.

No reply. Of course not. Of course there isn't. What am I thinking? What on earth am I doing?

I'm doing this because it's what Mum wanted. That's what I have to keep reminding myself. Mum planned all of this because we'd both found Dad's funeral so *unpleasant and upsetting.* Dazed with grief we were, though we knew it was coming. We let them prepare his body. We let the funeral directors take care of everything. And when we visited together, the night before his burial, Dad had looked so strange in the casket—in his rarely worn shiny suit, his skin plumped up and his cheeks garishly pink—that Mum had snorted when she saw him. Then she moaned. *That's not him. That's nothing like him.* The well-intentioned funeral director had nodded. *The dead* do *look different,* he'd said. *Sometimes seeing them can help you feel that they've* truly *departed. That's not what I mean,* my mother said to me, *that's not what I mean at all.* And then the funeral director proceeded to tell us that the casket was hardwood and would be sealed so that nothing could get in and the body would be well preserved. *And then how will he be food for worms?* she'd said. *I don't want him staying like* this. And the funeral director had had to explain that the process of embalming, of draining blood from the body and replacing it with formaldehyde, is irreversible, and that's what we'd paid for as part of the *Silver Package.* Things had gotten chaotic then, and I'd had to manage Mum out of the building.

Mum had wanted *me* to take care of her body—not strangers. And she wanted one last road trip. She'd heard a programme on the radio about it, about do-it-yourself burials, with your loved ones travelling in a caravan to bury you in a field. She didn't want to be embalmed. She didn't want to be sealed off. She'd heard about Tibetan sky burials, where the dead were left out on mountains to be eaten by birds. Failing that, she said, she'd at least like to be food for worms.

One problem with Mum having lived such a long time is that almost all her friends are already gone. Edna is the last one left. The afternoon light makes the windscreen a big golden smear. The trees on either side of the road are projecting new leaves, glossy little clutches of them at the ends of branches. I drive slowly down a wide avenue. Behind the high walls and gates, I try to sight the big houses. Formby is where the Liverpool footballers live, isn't it? And apparently also where Edna has ended up. Pinewoods Care Home is sign posted up ahead.

A receptionist directs me to the lounge. Edna is still recognisable: arched eyebrows, wild eyes, gaudy jumper. Her family must pay a fortune for this place—posh chairs in the reception, the nurses in smart uniforms. But once you're properly inside it's the same as where Mum was. There are wipe-clean chairs, the now-familiar, peppery tang of double incontinence.

Hello, Edna, I say. It's Lizzie, Doris's daughter. I phoned yesterday?

Edna stares at me, then squeezes her eyes almost closed.

I've brought Doris… to see you, like I said I would.

Does Edna remember our phone conversation? Does she even remember Mum?

Doris? Doris Parker? I haven't seen her in *years*.

A woman sitting in a chair close to us begins to groan.

She does this all the time, Edna says, giving her a sour look. Just lolls there. I don't know how they get her into those tights. Gone bovine, hasn't she?

Edna, I say, I'm not sure if you remember our conversation? Doris... passed away. Last week. This might seem strange, but I've brought her here. In my van. We're taking a trip. She didn't want a traditional funeral. But she wanted to come and see you. And I wondered if... you might want to... see her? Have a last cup of tea together?

Edna is looking at me suspiciously. Then she says: I'm not so good at my walking.

It's slow progress through the corridors of the building. Edna leans heavily on me. Once we're outside, she comes to a halt, face upturned, blinking in the cold light.

We're over here, I say, steering her towards the campervan.

I open the side door and pull down the step.

Now how am I supposed to get up there? she says.

We'll manage, I say.

I half-help, half-force Edna up the step, pushing her from behind.

But I should have gone in first, because the shroud-bundle is face-down on the floor, and Mum's bare feet and the backs of her calves are exposed. Well, this is undignified. And what's Edna going to make of it? Will it frighten her?

I'm sorry, Edna, I say.

Still, I don't touch Mum; I don't try to roll her over. It's not Edna who's afraid. It's me, isn't it?

Have a seat, Edna, I say. I'll put the kettle on. Would you like tea?

Them's her feet, then? They look... old. She makes the word 'old' long and grave.

Yes, I say. Ninety! What an amazing age to reach.

Well I'm ninety-one, Edna says.

I toss the teabags into the sink and take the seat next to Edna.

Edna slurps her tea. Your mum. Doris. She was always a bonny one. Was it bad... at the end? she asks.

What to say to that?

That Mum asked me to take her home again and again, and I couldn't. That I watched her face as she went. That the last inhale had been like a child's exhausted cry, the sound gone and the breath just a tremor. And then: nothing. No exhale. Thin bones, creased skin, pale eyelashes. Was it bad? Yes. Yes. It was awful—awful in its quiet inevitability. But not bad in the way Edna means.

It was peaceful at the end, I say. She talked about you a lot, Edna, these last few years.

Well, she didn't bloody write, Edna says.

Edna had sent cards to my mum, even at the home. Though there was not a lot written in them, sometimes just a scrawl, *Love Edna*, on the inside. They were tawdry cards decked with roses and gold writing, some of them wildly inappropriate: *With Sympathy* when there'd been no death; *Happy Fortieth Birthday*, when Doris had last been eighty-five. Occasionally there'd be a paragraph that started *Remember*, and she'd have written out some event or scene that meant nothing to me as I read it aloud, but Mum would laugh. Mum's laugh—a bolt of lightning that might illuminate a room or strike you down.

Well, she loved your cards, and so did I, I say. I read them to her. And I know she wanted to see you.

Well. Course she would, says Edna. There's no bugger else now.

Edna drinks her tea and then she bangs the cup down on the side table. I think I'd like to go back inside now. Yes, I would. You could catch your death out here.

Heading west for the night, towards the coast, and I'm wondering: Is that really the kind of meeting that Mum had had in mind when she planned this trip? When I returned Edna to the care of the Pinewoods nurses, she clawed at my cardigan when I made to leave, saying, *Why did you come, why did you bring her here, upsetting me like this?* And it briefly looked like things might turn nasty. I'd promised I'd see her again and that seemed to do the trick, though I feel bad about it now. I pacified her with false brightness.

Almost dark now. The road weaving through the woods. I pull the van up in the National Trust car park, swing it horizontally across several empty bays, so that the side-doors face the sand dunes. No one else here to bother about it. Mum longed to see the ocean when she was landlocked in the care home in Bingley; but things moved quickly and there had been no moving her after the last operation.

I'm jittery and I need to eat. The light is fading fast now. The sounds outside the van separate around us: the exhale of the waves, the kittiwakes crying themselves towards sleep.

I don't want to go into the back of the van.

We used to come out this way on holidays when I was young. To Morcombe, Blackpool, Southport. Mum loved this coast. When she was young, her whole family would come out to Blackpool, aunts and uncles and cousins staying in adjacent boarding houses. The mills and factories would shut for a fortnight and she would meet girls from school at the pleasure beach and spot folk from their street on the promenade. Half of Bradford went to Blackpool in August, she used to say.

This is what she wanted. This is what Mum wanted, isn't it? Even if it wasn't perfect with Edna. Even if I can't bring myself to touch her yet. And me too. I wanted this trip. God knows I didn't want a repeat of Dad's funeral.

Then why can't I bring myself to go back there to her?

In the mosque at the end of Mum's old street, I know that families sit with their dead—that they wash them in warm water and shroud them and stay close to them, taking turns through the night, keeping them company right until burial. When I researched Mum's plan, I found out about all sorts of different funeral rituals. In Colorado, bodies are prepared by the family with boughs of juniper. In Indonesia, people preserve the dead and keep them at home—they talk to them, children even sleep beside them, they're looked after by the family until the money is raised for the funeral. In Tibet, bodies are prepared for sky burial by hand, pounded and chopped by loved ones in readiness for the birds.

Why, then, is it so hard for me to go back there?

I turn on the radio. I make myself climb into the back of the van and switch on the lamps and I eat two packets of crisps and wash them down with a bottle of brown ale and I don't look at her naked feet. When the light's out and I've killed the radio, I feel so, so afraid. But Christ, I can't leave her face-down like that for the whole night. I get off the couch. I feel for her in the dark. She's cold. Cold even through the cotton shroud. Emanating cold. I roll her. I roll her onto her back. Then I lay my blanket over her.

When I lie back down on the couch, I can feel the fear returning.

Some say that he died of a fever/ Some say that he died of a fright.

Whenever I was scared at night and called for her, she'd come. *Now then, Lizzie. Do you need singing to?*

I was raised by fearless women. My mother's mother, Florrie, lived for almost a century at the end of our road and arseholed anyone—man or beast—who stepped out of line. One story my mother often told about her: When my uncle John was a boy, he'd returned home from school and attempted to conceal something. Florrie, sharp-eyed, saw that he couldn't hold his cup of tea properly and made him extend his left arm in front of her. It was shaking. He'd been caned badly across his palm for using his left hand to write. Now Florrie, who couldn't read and write well herself, wasn't going to let anyone get in the way of her children learning. She'd taken John to school the next morning herself and shouted for his teacher to come out. When the woman refused, she hauled her out of the classroom by her bun while the children whooped in the playground and then she gave her the dressing down of her life. Florrie's fearlessness was legendary. And my mum inherited it. I feared her anger like nothing else. Once, when I was still a small girl and walking home from school, I was flashed at by a man on the corner of our street and ran home in tears—I was upset less by the loose pink junk that was shaken at me and more by the wild leer on the man's face. When my mother had had the story out of me, she armed herself with the kitchen scissors and a rolling pin and ran back out onto the road, bellowing for him and knocking on every door. I prayed that he'd made a quick getaway.

That same nerve must be buried somewhere in me, surely? Ferocity in the bone marrow? Will fearlessness advance in me with age, like the menopause and bladder cancer and osteoporosis?

*

I wake with the dawn. I almost trip over Mum getting out of bed. Sorry, Mum. Sorry. I wash, scrawl on some lipstick, and jump out of the side of the van. A pair of red squirrels are stock-still at the edge of the woods. They're tiny creatures, with ludicrous tawny tufts rising high from each ear and fat white stomachs. They look like rats wearing miniature reindeer suits. I laugh and they skitter off into the woods.

We make good time on the drive south and arrive at the edge of London by late morning. I have to circle the streets a few times to find a space big enough for the van. Once I'm parked up, I call Grace on the mobile.

You're early, Grace says.

Yes, I was lucky with the traffic. Shall I come to you or do you want to come out to us?

Us? Oh Christ, Mum, come here. Just give me two minutes.

I climb down from the van, wanting to stretch my legs. Grace lives on a handsome street of tall sandstone Victorian terraces. Some of the houses haven't even been broken up into flats—front gardens with clusters of daffodils in the ground and cyclamens in pots. I walk up the path to Grace's flat. Not looking too bad. Some primroses and narcissi in the patch of ground here. I ring the doorbell and there is a slight delay before Grace appears, wet hair hanging down either side of her face. Sometimes it takes the breath right out of me when I see her again after a while. That strong rush that I feel to touch her, but the way in which she also looks like a stranger.

She ushers me into the flat without embracing me.

I was going to cook, Mum, but I didn't have time because you're early. So Haroon's making us some sandwiches.

I had digestives for breakfast and I'm absolutely ravenous.

That's fine, love, I say. Not to worry. How are you?

Grace sits cross-legged on the sofa and begins to wind a strand of wet hair between her fingers. I can hear the foot-steps of a man in the flat above us.

Did you sleep in the van with her? Grace asks.

Yes. Yes, love, I did. Your nan and I—

Mum, it's weird. I can't... I don't want to talk about it.

But you asked, Grace—

Haroon comes through in a tracksuit with a plate full of egg sandwiches.

Hello, Mrs Parker. I'm sorry to hear about your loss.

He stands before me and offers out the sandwiches. I take three.

Thank you, Haroon. That's kind of you.

Grace shakes her head when offered the plate.

Dad says you've lost it again, she says. Doing this... weird journey. Shouldn't we all be at a proper funeral?

She begins to cry then.

Oh, Grace, I say.

I put the sandwiches on my lap. I reach out a hand towards her, but she turns away from me. When she was small, Grace would climb into tiny spaces whenever she was upset: the void under a chair, the corner of a wardrobe. I could never work out if she was trying to hide from the hurt or barricade herself in with it against me.

This is what your nan wanted, love, I say. She was very specific. She wanted to go on a last journey, and she particularly wanted to come to see you. She would have loved to have seen you set up in this flat. Come out to the van and you can say a proper goodbye to her.

I don't know... I don't know if I... can, Mum.

She's stopped crying now so I decide to change tack. I'll try to establish some sort of normalcy.

Okay, I say, Well there's no rush. Let's think about it, shall we. How's work going?

It's... you know, she says. Manic. Actually, I'm thinking of retraining. I know how much *you* loved teaching. But it's just... it's totally different now. The admin and the scrutiny and the levels of support the kids need. I can't get any proper help for my SEN lot.

Yes, I say, I can imagine. I try to sound as neutral as possible. So what might you do instead?

I've been thinking of training to teach Alexander technique. Dad has said he'll help.

Oh, I say. Right. Alexander technique. And what is that exactly?

Grace sighs. I knew you'd be like this, she says. If I could tell you exactly what it is, then I wouldn't need to do the training, would I?

I don't know how to reply to this. I upset Grace in ways I can never predict.

We don't have any dessert, Grace says. Because you came early.

Then she starts to cry again, properly this time—sobbing. I move towards her. I sit right next to her and put my arms around her.

Grace, I say. Love. It's okay. It's okay.

I rock her until she rubs her face with her palms and shakes me off.

Okay, she says. Okay. I'll come out to the van with you.

When we get up into the back of the van, I'm not sure what to do. Mum is lying on the floor, right side up, with the shroud over her face. Grace has folded her arms and is gripping them tightly.

Would you like tea? I ask.

Grace shakes her head.

We both sit down on the couch.

Would you like to... touch her? I ask. Or to say something to her?

I'm... I'm not sure, she says. What does she look like now, Mum?

Well, I say carefully, I've been... a bit nervous about seeing her myself. There will be some... changes. But she won't be... stiff at least.

What, you mean you haven't looked at her face?

I shake my head.

Oh, Grace says. Mum. We'd better do that, hadn't we? If that's what Nan wanted? If she wanted us to *see* her to say goodbye?

I nod.

Grace kneels down next to Mum. She hesitates, her hands hovering in front of her. Then she takes hold of the white fabric shroud and begins to fold it downwards to reveal Mum's face.

Mum's eyes are closed. Her lashes have paled to nothing. Her face is not uniformly colourless any more; her lips, her nose, her throat—they're starting to purple. I know that in a couple of days her stomach will begin to bloat. The body is only still for a short time before it erupts into new forms of life.

But just now, she is quiet. My mum who was never quiet. She looks perfectly, awfully still. She is so quiet that she looks as though she has never lived. She doesn't look dead in the way that I feared. She doesn't look like a person who has died. She looks like something different entirely. Something new: an elderly stillborn.

Grace whispers something to her that I can't hear. Afterwards, I go with Grace back into the flat to use the bathroom. My hands are shaking, but I try not to let Grace see. We hug and then Haroon shows me to the door. He leans in towards me as I turn to go.

I think what you're doing is really cool, Mrs Parker, he says. Then he steps back into the hallway.

The final stage of the drive is the longest. I always forget how far this stretch of land at the bottom of England extends into the sea. And how the south-west is a different country, with its own language. I drive past signs for Kilivose, Gwithian, Phillack, Gwinear. This is where Mum will rest, buried in a field in Cornwall, feeding the earth. Her body will be recomposed—composting clover and creeping buttercup and speedwell.

This is also where Patricia moved nearly a decade ago to start her new life in Carbis Bay. We haven't spoken much since then. But we send letters and cards at Christmas, and when I rang and told her about Mum she knew exactly what to do. She found a farmer who had a field set aside for natural burials and sorted everything.

I feel antsy driving towards Tricia. It's a skittish feeling, as though I might shy away from the hurdle and drive straight on, straight past Tricia's house, headstrong, into the sea. I'm still shaky from seeing Mum's face. And what will it be like between me and Tricia now? Ten years is a long time. When we were both still married, we saw each other every week. Tricia had her boy, Jake, the same year that Grace was born and we met at a group—the Group for Desperate Mothers, we used to call it. We shared our observations as Grace and Jake grew. We frightened each other with worries, then reassured each other. We pooled our frustrations. We took wine to the park in flasks and I saved up everything to tell Tricia. But it hadn't been the same for her, had it? Because she didn't tell me the most important thing, did she?

Here we go. I pull up outside Tremayne Cottage. This hill start is going to be a right bugger. Tricia's house is on a narrow road that rises steeply from the beach. It's a handsome white bungalow with shuttered windows and a veranda that looks out to sea. The rest of the hillside is terraced with enormous white properties, many of them guest houses and hotels. Tricia must have sold her stake in the veterinary practice for a pretty penny. There's a figure at the window, waving at me, then flickering out of view. I glance at myself in the rear-view mirror. I'll have to do.

We sit in wicker seats in the lounge, facing the ocean. Tricia has made us strong gin and tonics and the sun is setting, dazzling across the sea. There is a man walking a spaniel across the sand. Tricia is quiet even though she's on to her second drink. She's cut her hair, so now it falls in a heavy bob onto her shoulders and it's turned completely grey—a colour like oyster shells. Her face is tanned and lithe. Jasmine is making us dinner in the kitchen, and occasionally calls through to Tricia: Baby, do we have cilantro? Baby, where's the red wine?

The appellation makes Tricia wince. It's almost imperceptible, but I spot it—a little flinch in her shoulders.

I down my drink.

Thank you, I say, for sorting everything out.

I'm happy to have been able to, she says. And at least it means I finally get to see you.

I wish I'd visited before, I say. I never meant to leave things so long.

We've invited you, Tricia says. Every year—

I know, I say. I know. I can't explain it.

Because now that I'm near her again, now that I see the glint of hurt that I've created, I wonder what on earth I was playing at. It was me, not her, wasn't it? Why did I do it? Why did I cut her off like that?

Both of our marriages had frayed apart as our children had grown. I'd told her everything along the way, and I thought she'd told me everything too. When I found out about Steve and Janet, it was Tricia I'd wanted to see. I'd gotten home from work to find that the post was still on the mat. I'd gone to hang up my coat and there it was, bold as brass: a thin silk scarf in turquoise and pink. I recognised it immediately. It had been left behind by Janet, a member of the bridge club Steve had joined. Janet had the very worst taste in scarves—they were always gauzy, lurid affairs. She dressed as though she was auditioning to present something on the Shopping Channel. I walked about the kitchen, back and forth. I opened a cupboard door, mindlessly, then slammed it shut again. It was so careless of them, so insultingly careless to leave the evidence right there. And yet: this felt so good. There was a wonderfully violent current rippling through me. This was it! Things were going to change now. This was what I'd needed.

And the person I wanted to go to then was Tricia. I'd wanted to talk to her, to hammer it all out. I knew she would be at the hustings in town—she'd cancelled our dinner date to go. I would walk there to see her, that was what I would do. I stormed out the front door. Then I came back in again for my handbag. I was lightheaded. I was giddy with excitement! I took a moment to check myself: handbag, coat, keys. I stormed out again!

I walked with furious momentum, thinking about nothing except how good it felt to put one foot in front of the other, to pound my feet against the earth to travel towards Tricia. I slid in at the back of the town hall. There were three men on the stage. One of them was talking about refuse collection. There weren't very many people in the audience. I took a seat and scanned for Tricia, finding her long, heavy grey-blonde hair just a few rows ahead. She was sitting next to a woman I didn't know, a younger woman with dark skin and short hair. The woman's neck was totally exposed, her hair razored close at the back. There was something singular about the way Tricia's body was angled towards the younger woman's, and the round, regular movement in Tricia's shoulder. Tricia's arm was laced around the other woman. Tricia had her right hand on the bottom of the woman's back, and she was slowly and firmly kneading around the other woman's hips. Tricia was *caressing* this woman. And something about her touch, about the careful way she worked her hands, made me think that the unknown woman must be menstruating. Tricia was easing the places where her hands felt the hurt.

I bolted from the meeting.

My life changed entirely then. I locked Steve out of the house. I refused to meet with Tricia and refused to give her a reason. Grace was furious with me. Steve said I was having a breakdown. And something was changing with Mum. She was having problems recognising people, and her strength would suddenly fail her. She looked at me incredulously when she couldn't remember something or her legs gave way, as if to say, *Well, who's this incomer then?*

One night Tricia's husband fetched up red-eyed on my doorstep. Tricia was leaving him. She was moving to Cornwall to work as a veterinary locum. She was selling up her part of the practice. *I can't understand it*, he mewled at me across the dining table. *She's seemed so much happier these last few months. Hasn't she?* And then he looked at me with some excitement. *Do you think divorce might be contagious, Liz? That she got the idea from you? Perhaps you could talk some sense into her? Tell her how... miserable it is?* He motioned towards the half-packed boxes that surrounded us, and then towards me, swaddled in my intermittently soiled dressing gown.

I sorted everything out that needed to be sorted. The house was sold and Mum's house too. I moved into a flat in town and I settled Mum into the first care home. Once I'd dealt with all the paperwork, finalised things with Steve through the solicitors, painted walls and put up shelves, sorted out all of Mum's belongings, done every possible necessary practical thing, my mind turned back to Tricia. She'd written to me with a new address: *Patricia Mundy and Jasmine Williams at Tremayne Cottage.* How could I not have known? I'd told her everything, every significant detail of my life. But she'd kept this a secret from me. Why? Because it was another woman she'd fallen in love with? I thought again and again of that caress, of the way Tricia had touched Jasmine. I thought of how Jasmine's body might have felt, the way my body used to feel every month—as though a series of internal knots had formed in my abdomen. I thought of Tricia's hands gently, relentlessly, working them loose. No one had ever caressed me that way.

I felt livid with envy. And I felt bereft.

Everyone I had loved was becoming a stranger.

We eat in the kitchen. Jasmine has made us Cajun fish, rice and salad, and the food is delicious. Jasmine is American. She is curt and she doesn't smile much. She ignores my attempts at compliments—which is fair enough. But her face comes to life when she looks at Tricia. Tricia tells us a grim but funny story about her day locuming and having to pick maggots out of a rabbit's genitals with tweezers and the rabbit then peeing in her face.

Ha! Jasmine shouts. Poor baby!

When we've finished dinner, Tricia says, What about seeing Doris, then? I'd like to say goodbye.

I'm lightheaded. The combination of adrenaline and gin: it makes me want to rush at Tricia, to hold her close until she can feel how sorry I am.

Okay, I say. Yes, let's go out to the van.

When we're outside, I reach for Tricia's hand. The night air here smells different. There's a palm tree crackling in the breeze.

I open the door of the van and turn on the light.

It's a surprise, somehow, to see Mum still there where I left her, her face exposed.

She's so very still.

I falter. I almost stumble backwards.

Are you ok? Tricia says.

She closes the door behind us and puts her arm around my waist.

It's just... it's still a shock, sometimes. To see her like this.

I think she looks rather stately, Tricia says. Sepulchral. Put your kettle on then.

I turn away to make the tea and Tricia sits down.

Teaspoons, measuring out, stirring. These small, concrete movements are good to focus on.

We'll come with you to the site tomorrow, she says. Help you prepare things?

That's kind of you, I say. Really. But Mum set it all out. It should be just her and me there.

The digging will be hard work, you know.

I know, I say, but I need to do it alone.

We sit for a while without speaking. I'm restless again. I want to be doing something, though I can't say what.

I'll need to be off early, I say. So I'll say goodbye to you both tonight.

Alright, Tricia says. If you're sure. Help yourself to anything you need before you go.

I've finished my tea. What will I do now? What do you do the night before you dig your mother's grave?

Will you sleep in the house with us? Tricia asks.

No, I say. No, I want to be with her these last... couple of nights.

That word—*last*—catches right in my throat.

Tricia puts her arm around me and I rest my cheek on her shoulder.

Come back, she says. Won't you? Come back to visit us again?

I will, I say. I promise I will.

Is it okay, Tricia says, if I touch her?

Yes, I say.

Tricia kneels down next to Mum. She doesn't seem afraid or even perturbed. She must deal with death a lot. Veterinary work is mostly euthanasia, she told me once. Tricia is looking at Mum's face. Then she reaches out, sweeps the hair back from Mum's forehead, as if touching her body is the most natural thing in the world, and she lets her hand rest against Mum's cold cheek.

She leans in and whispers, Sleep well now, Doris.

This is what digging is like: at first, I cut the turf away in neat squares. The spade cinches through the topsoil easily and there is a gratifying regularity to the work and to stacking the clods together. At first, the soil moves quite easily—dandelions give way to a writhing substrate of worms and grubs, and the earth is loose and black and loamy. There are some long roots to dig out—hairy dock tubers curled into the earth. Then the real graft starts. I dig down into the denser ground, into the seams of clay. There's rock there too, large chunks that jar my back when the spade hits them.

The farmer supplied me with the spade and a mattock and supports, and with instructions for finding the plot and measuring out the dimensions. He inspected my certificates, then asked me to sign some forms. He had none of the customer-service gloss of funeral directors. *Who's digging then?* he'd asked. *Just me,* I replied. He looked sceptical then. *Likely you won't get it all done before the rain,* he said and handed over the equipment.

I've been at it for hours when the muscles in my lower back begin to spasm. Maybe he was right. Maybe I won't be able to get it done in time. I'm not even at half the required depth and every swing of the spade is a shudder through my shoulders and the joints of my hands and the balls of my feet. I should have thought of this and worn thicker soles.

I lie down in the damp grass for a while, and then I begin again.

Mid-afternoon, inside the half-grave, still digging, and a man appears in the bottom corner of the field. He squats close to the ground, then turns on his haunches to watch me. I'm close to delirious from the digging. The sweat covering me is frothing under my clothes. I haven't eaten since 6 a.m. My arms are shaking. I throw down the spade. Christ's sake. This is impossible. I climb out of the hole. I kick one of the rocks I've unearthed. Then I sit down and let my body hang forwards between my legs. Everything hurts. I allow myself one short, dry, exhausted cry. When I look up, the man is advancing towards me.

Bloody hell. He'll think it's a plea for help.

I get back on my feet and jump down into the grave.

A few moments later, and he's next to me, holding his hat in place against the breeze.

Hello, he says.

Hi, I say, but I don't stop digging.

Are you doing this by yourself?

Yes, I say. Looks like it, doesn't it?

And this is all the equipment you've got?

Yep.

It'll be getting dark soon, you know.

Yes! I say. And I've a lot to do!

I hadn't meant to shout. I push my hair out of my face and I can feel that I've smeared earth across my forehead.

Right, the man says. He turns away and starts to walk back down the field.

I didn't mean... I call after him. But I don't know what I didn't mean.

The man pauses, back still turned to me. Then he carries on walking, right to the bottom of the field and out of the thicket pass. I hear his car drive away.

Digging. More digging. Slicing through the wet clay, hitting against stone again and again. Occasional unidentifiable objects down here. A grey, curved, pock-marked thing: the jaw of an old sheep, perhaps? My movements are small and slow now, and when I stand up I am up to my ribcage in grave. I try to claw the soil away around a particularly large rock. I sit in the grave and tear at the earth. My hands are freezing and the light is dropping quickly.

The man in the hat reappears at the bottom corner of the field. He's walking the hypotenuse towards me again, carrying a rucksack and two large tool-bags. I stand up in the grave and watch him approach.

I'm sorry, I say when he's close enough to hear.

You needn't apologise, the man says. He puts his bags down on the ground. It's bloody hard work. If you're trying to get through it today, you'll need something to eat.

He fetches two pasties, half a cling-filmed cherry cake, a flask and cups from his rucksack, and places them between us.

A few other things that might help too, he says. And he positions two lights, like big, flat fish-eyes, beside the grave. He unfolds a metal step-stool. And finally, he throws a pair of old, soiled gardening gloves down on the ground.

I clamber out of the grave.

Help yourself, he says.

Will you join me? I ask.

Happily, he says. We both sit down on the grass. He unscrews the top of the flask and pours out two cups of coffee.

I stretch my legs. All my muscles are ticking. My body feels like the sound the van's engine makes as it cools down. I eat hungrily, not able to stop myself from going first.

That's my dad down there, the man says. I know exactly where he is without measuring because that's where the orange-peel fungus is growing. He was six-foot-four. Think yourself lucky it's a small grave.

Yes, Mum's tiny, I say. I didn't think... I didn't realise how difficult the digging would be.

Oh, no, it's back-breaking work. There were three of us doing Dad's and it took most of a day, and then most of the next to refill it. You'll need to make mud pies, you know, when you cover her?

Yes, the farmer told me, I say. Important to make the mud dense, he said, to *keep out the bigger beasts.*

Will you bury your mother tonight?

No, I say, I'd like to do it at dawn. If I manage to get it finished in time.

You're almost there, says the man. You're in the campervan?

I nod.

Look, my wife and I live just over there. He points at the wooded hill beyond the field. The cottage on the bend of the road. You might have passed it? In case you need anything. And when you've finished tomorrow, whatever time it is, just come and drop the stuff back off with us. You can park up in our drive and sleep there if you like. Have a bath and something hot to eat.

That's kind of you, I say. Thank you.

I dig as the dark thickens. When I stand up straight, I'm submerged in the grave, the earth at the height of my heart. The lamps on either side make a circle of light above me. Beyond that there's the night sky, a dense black arc, full of careering animal sounds: whistling, screeching, warbled lamentations. I'm surrounded by clay too, by the wet, dark stink of it. The cold from the earth travels up through my boots into my bones. *It has to be as deep as your chest*, the farmer said to me. *Then you're done*. I'm done. I throw the spade up and back onto the ground, then feel around for the step that the man left me. I hadn't thought about how I would get out once the grave was finished. The kindness of strangers.

When I wake, it's still dark. Have I slept at all? My body feels extraordinary. Every muscle is lagged with the effort of digging.

I put the kettle on and look out of the small window next to the stove. The light is just beginning. The sky is splitting open above the hills, the night torn through with gold.

After I've drunk the tea, I kneel down on the floor next to Mum and I look at her face. I don't turn on the lamp yet. I kneel right next to her and touch her cold cheek with my palm and then my fingertips. Then I pull the shroud all the way up, so that her face is gone. I kiss her through the thin white cotton, and I begin to sing.

But it's her voice. It's her voice that I hear—thick and glitchy, and always right beside me whenever I feel afraid.

Cluster

The man two doors down pursues a secret hobby in the dead of night. This is one of your first discoveries.

You haven't slept at all. The nightlight is a small crescent of brightness in the dark blur of milk and skin and adrenaline that night has become. Then there is this sound intruding from the world outside. A clang as something drops to the ground. Metal against concrete. Scuffling, mechanistic clacking. None of these noises would be loud enough to wake you if you were fast asleep. But in this new nocturnal world, they are insistent and intimate—in the same way that voices on the phone whorl into your ear, closer even than someone speaking next to you.

You glance at your phone, which now sleeps under the corner of your pillow. Tilt it, make it glow. Three twenty-five. There have been letters from the police, opened by Ola in the flat downstairs and left on the table in the shared hallway—letters about burglaries in the area. You should get out of bed and check on the sounds. But even the thought of witnessing a crime is poor motivation. You force yourself to move. You rise up, move past the Moses basket to the window. You open the curtain just a fraction. Out there are parallel lines of backyards and the black river of cobbles that bisects them.

You wait for another sound. And it comes again: the jangle of metal. You survey the terraces. Two doors down, there's a small Tilley lamp at the end of the yard and a man crouched down beside it. It takes a while for the scene to sharpen into coherence. A man is crouching over a wheel, spinning it. A bike is upside down, and the man stoops over it, working on something at the wheel-hub, adjusting it, then spinning the wheel again. You watch for a while longer. The man's movements are slow and full of care. He works over the body of the bike with a soft cloth. He stands back and puts his hands in his pockets. You let the curtain fall back into place. All this detail, all this secret work, folded back into the dark.

After that, you listen for him in the night-time when the baby frets and whinnies awake, over and over, startling out of sleep as though she is falling, falling, into something terrible, her tiny limbs twitching, her mouth a worried beak—the baby who does not yet know what sleep is, who does not know its softness. You listen for the man when you scoop the baby up and rock her and try to teach her how to sleep, whilst beginning to forget how to yourself. You listen for him moving around and for his hidden industry. He is your new co-worker in the night-time economy.

♦

Ali sleeps. He sleeps through all of it, even those first few nights at home with the baby. How can he? The baby makes such noises, such awful tiny rasps and rattles and sighs, as though breathing is altogether too difficult, as though she might give up on it at the turn of each breath. Fifteen days old now, the creature at your breast. The nightlight glances off her darting eyes; half-blind eyes that can barely see beyond your face, but they flicker wildly when she latches at your breast, as though she is checking sideways for competition or predators. You hear scuffling outside. The secret mechanic, you think at first. But no—this isn't him. The scuffling is more persistent and less careful tonight. There is laughter, and then there are low voices. Earlier there was bellowing and singing: voices of people veering in the street as they stumbled home from the pub.

It's Friday night, you remind yourself. The weeks have lost their shape now that the night-time lasts so much longer than the day. But today you took the baby to a class, a class for new mothers in the city centre, so you know that it was Friday today. At the end of the class there had been an opportunity to ask questions. You'd all sat in a circle on beanbags, your babies bundled at your chests. The other women looked variously blissful or alarmed or stupefied by the arrival of the creatures in their arms. *I read a story about a bottle of baby powder exploding and the baby choking to death on the dust*, one woman said. *Is it true? Can talcum powder kill them? Am I not supposed to be powdering him? God*, another woman had said, *there are stories about everything. Try not to read them. This one's my second, and the older one—she's five—she came home from school yesterday and said, 'Mum, what's a terrorist?' Just you wait until that happens, then you can really start to worry. This is the easy bit.* Some of the other women in the circle had begun to fidget then, to shift uncomfortably on their beanbags, whether from their episiotomies or from the talk of terrorism or from the thought of all of this being easy, it was difficult to say. You resolved to never go to a mums' group again.

The voices outside continue. The baby is still at your breast. The baby has been at your breast all night long. *Cluster feeding*, the health visitor who led the group had explained, *is very common in the early days. The baby might feed for hours in the night. Hours and hours. It's clever. It knows when to seek its mother out, with the best chance of her undivided attention. With the best chance of her body guarding it against the cold, and snakes, and raiders.*

But we don't have snakes in South Leeds, do we? one dazed-looking girl had said. *Oh, no, dear,* the health visitor said, *I'm speaking ev-o-lut-ion-arily.*

Cluster. The new word flickers in your mind as the baby's face repeatedly shivers into your breast, searching and finding. Clustering. Cluster fuck. Cluster bomb. Cluster headache. None of these associations are exactly encouraging.

You listen again for the voices outside. There's a bit of back and forth out there. Some sort of negotiation is taking place. You scoop the baby up, keeping her latched, when you finally move to the window. You open the curtain a fraction. There are three of them in the back alley, three lads. Two of them are jittering about, moving from foot to foot, pushing hands into pockets, taking them out again, pushing them back in. The other man is making a show of not being nervous. He's wearing a bulky jacket and he leans back into the light cast by the streetlamp at the very end of the alley so that he can count their money. He's selling. He passes something over to one of the lads. Then he's off, leaving the pair of them to lean into one another, to unwrap their tiny tinfoil parcel.

This network of Victorian alleys at the edge of the city is a gift for buyers and sellers. There are often needles in the gutters. Ola has called for an ambulance on several occasions, for young lads and old men alike, not able to make it home before necking what they've bought. *What city doesn't have a drug problem?* Ali said, when you looked around the place. *And anyway, that's why we can afford a nice flat with a proper double-bedroom, right, so let's not knock it?* You're not knocking it now. You're glad of the company, however anonymous, while the baby *clusters*. You return to bed and lean back on the pillows. The baby tilts back her head, swooning with milk. You listen as the lads stagger off together.

♦

Sometimes there is singing. There's a couple whose voices you begin to recognise. They stumble home together from the pub a couple of nights a week. They're both hoarse and boisterous. Some nights they sing together, nineties Britpop anthems, blundering through the words, compensating for inaccuracy with volume. Tonight, it's mostly the woman singing. Her voice cracks when she reaches for the high notes. You don't recognise the song. The man whoops when she finishes. Their voices recede and the street settles back into quiet. In the distance, a freight train is accelerating away from the city like sound travelling down a mineshaft. Silence. A siren. The whoosh of the motorway picked up by the wind. Silence. When the baby finally falls asleep in your arms, you are too afraid of waking her to even try to lay her down.

♦

A blackbird breaks the quiet outside. When you check your phone, dawn is still far off. The bird is misfiring in the dark. That's another of your discoveries: the sounds of birds. You listen to them now as daybreak approaches each morning. There are so many of them, calling out to each other across the rooftops, telling one another of the light beginning on the horizon. You've begun looking for them in the daytime too, trying to identify them. There's a pair of blackbirds nesting in the privet at the front. They seem to be doing things so carefully and equitably. The nest is hidden inside the hedge and each parent, when it is time to exit the nest, darts out suddenly, leaving any watcher uncertain of the location of the chicks. When a parent returns, they initially stand some way off, on the top of the gatepost for example, with a morsel in beak, checking and checking once again that no one can see where they are about to go. You watch this from the front window as you pace with the baby, you watch the birds take turns all day long, so prudent and so diligent.

They're wise to be careful. The mangey white cat from next door—its fur yellowed at the paws as if by a nicotine habit—waits on the doorstep, licking its claws. Over the road, where the houses have small front gardens, two ducks have made their nest a surprising distance from the river. A clutch of thirteen eggs is hidden underneath a shrub. The man whose garden they have chosen fills an ice-cream container each day with water for them, and sometimes the dawn chorus admits some quacking. Yesterday afternoon, the old man stopped you on your walk out with the pram to tell you that a plumber's merchant had run over the drake—

the man had to scrape him off the road with a spade—and now the female is circling her eggs dementedly, giving the whole game away. The foxes will surely come. What should he do, the man asked you, as though the pram qualified you in some way to give advice on expected ducklings. *I don't know*, you'd said. *What can you do?*

You tried not to think about the ducks as you walked the streets, the baby whimpering under gunmetal skies. But now that the blackbird has gone off at this early hour, you can't help but think of the nest. Can a blackbird be insomniac? Or is something afoot? Is the fox about, stalking the duck's eggs? All is quiet again. The baby is drowsing with milk. A memory materialises in the dark—of an experiment you were forced to take part in at primary school. Each of you is given an egg at the start of morning class. You are asked to keep it safe. The task is to try to guard it all day long, and the lesson is about the difficulty of looking after something precious and fragile, and about how much care is needed. Most girls put the eggs in their skirt pockets, their fingers curved around their cargo, hoping to see it through to the end. You make it to lunchtime, when a brief lapse in concentration and a desire for more pudding results in you leaning over and crushing the shell against the serving table. You drop the cracked egg into the dining-room bin then, with the slop of leftover custard and chocolate sponge. One girl in your group, Leanne, whose life is already marked by loss, smashed her egg almost immediately, hurling it against the playground wall. *I'll only end up breaking it*, she'd said, *might as well do it now.*

♦

It's the couple again, on their way home from the pub. Tonight they're heckling each other mercilessly. It's the woman you hear first. She's jeering, almost singing her insults at him.

The thing about you, yeah, is that you don't know when to shut up, do you? On and on about boring shit. No wonder Paul left. On and on about your dogs. No one cares about your pedigree bitch, Johnny.

She shrieks. Her heels clatter; she's stumbling around, winded by laughter.

Yeah, well the thing about you is that you don't have your own friends, do you, love? You're only friends with the blokes you're shagging, aren't you? Not exactly known for your conversation are you?

His voice is lower and rougher, but it's still got a playground, sing-song cadence.

Yeah, yeah, well at least I don't walk funny. Look at you, look at the fucking state of you! Bow-legged, walking like you're from Manchester, she shouts back.

Yeah, right, then why are you coming home with me, love? You can't get enough of my amble. And look at the state of you anyway. Look at that fucking fringed monstrosity you're carrying. What is it they say about handbags? Meant to be like a girl's cunt, aren't they?

Peals of laughter. Howling. Singing. Silence.

♦

In the middle of the night, in the time before, if you found yourself awake for long stretches, you would sometimes get to thinking about dying. *Imagine*, your brother used to say to you when you were a child, late at night, a torch up-lighting his nostrils and teeth, *imagine, our Ri, how many people have died in this house.* You grew up in a back-to-back in Meanwood, on the other side of the city. *It's over a hundred years old, you know, this house. And you know those meat-hooks in the cellar? Do you think they were only used for animals? And what was that creak in the hallway, Ri?*

But tonight, as you lie awake listening to the baby scratching the sides of the crib-basket, you don't wonder about who has died in this house. You think instead about how many people might have been born inside it. How many tiny creatures have spluttered into life, here, in front of the old fireplace or drenching the sheets of an old bed? People seldom give their consent to die, but no one can ever give their consent to being drawn into life. And endings seem more comprehensible, somehow, than something beginning. After all, no one is entirely responsible for death; even a murder is only foreshortening. But a birth? Conjuring something into being, into blood and bone and nails? You are truly culpable for that.

♦

The girl in the flat next door goes out every Thursday night. There is music beforehand. Several girls meeting there together—laughter, screaming, ferocious and repetitive swearing. Sometimes, in the early hours, you hear the girl return, closing the front door carefully, padding up the stairs to her flat, starting a film on her laptop, American voices pinging at one another indistinctly through the party wall.

Tonight, the girl returns with another girl. You are feeding the baby. You have been feeding the baby for more than an hour. The baby rests briefly, her head lolling back, and you think that you might be able to lie down, to rest for just a minute or two, but then her head lifts again, her eyes still closed like a bat's as she blindly latches back on, still hungry, clustering her small, soft mouth again.

Ali turns suddenly in the bed, sighs, settles back into sleep. You listen to the girls next door as you continue to feed. They are trying to whisper, but their voices speed each other along, rising, giggling, then shrieking. Eventually they taper off into silence—only to re-emerge before the dawn as long, soft, lush moans.

♦

It's the couple on the street again. The baby has just gone down in the basket when you hear shouting. They're rowing. The man's louder than he has been before. There's no laughter and the woman's not making any comebacks. By the time they're close to the house, he's going full throttle.

Don't think I don't know about it. Don't you stop here, don't you think you can stop here, don't you think you're not going to get what you deserve. Get up. Get up. You can fucking walk and you know what's coming to you.

You move to the window, push aside the curtain. Someone turns a light on in the house opposite.

They can call the fucking police. I don't give a fuck.

The woman's down on the pavement. She's in tight white jeans and a white top that has ridden up as she's dragged along. She's not making any sound: she's playing dead, trying to make herself as heavy as possible.

Fucking get up, you cunt. Stop putting it on.

Stay on the line, another voice in the darkness says to you. The police are on their way. Can you keep them in your sight?

I'm inside my flat, you say, and they've just started moving again.

Can you go outside? the voice asks calmly. Can you follow them at a safe distance?

You turn to the Moses basket. The baby is asleep. Ali is asleep too. But he'd hear, surely he'd hear the baby and he'd wake if anything were really wrong? If the baby needed him?

You can go outside. You can leave them together for just a moment. The idea is terrible and wonderful.

I'll try, you say.

You throw on your coat and shoes in the hallway and leave as quickly as you can. You can't have taken even a minute but when you open the door, there's no sound. The couple has vanished. You step out onto the street and the night is as black and cool and deep as an ocean. You walk up and down the road, check the turn-offs and the mouths of ginnels. But there's no sign of them.

I've lost them, you tell the call handler. I'm so sorry, I've lost them.

Can you keep checking? the voice says. We've had a number of calls. The police are almost with you.

There are lights on in some of the houses around you. Other people have called too. Other people have been awake, or woken, and heard. You turn back towards your flat. The sky above it is clear, the stars glinting coldly. This is the first time you have been outside alone since the baby arrived. You feel giddy. And you feel bereft.

You linger for a little longer on the street, even though the trail's gone cold. You think of the woman, somewhere close by but hidden from you. Will somebody else hear her again, someone who can help? Maybe there's someone listening for the woman right now, someone who will answer when she cries out, wherever she is.

You think of the first time you heard the baby's heartbeat in the blackness inside you: your own slow pulse answered by this new one, quickening. You listened for her so intently, with such care, hearing her inside yourself long before you saw her.

A police van is approaching. You flag it down.

They were heading that way and then I lost them, you say. She was wearing white. I'm sorry. I'm sorry.

♦

The call of an owl breaks through the night. At the same time, the baby laughs in her sleep, a goofy breathy laugh, her cheeks dimpling, her lips wet with milk. Your heart feels like it might be about to shatter.

You cry often these days. *Maybe it's that thing they talked about in the class, Ri, the baby blues,* Ali said last week when a photo on your phone of a friend and her baby and her mother all together set you off. *You could ask the doctor about it. Or we could try to find your mum again. The baby might help, you know, if she actually sees her. Help her to sort herself out, I mean. If she ever wants a proper relationship with her granddaughter. But whatever, we have a beautiful, healthy girl, Ri, there's nothing to be sad about.*

But it's not sadness. Not exactly. The thing is, you now think, the thing is that you've lost all of your conditioning. You learned about Pavlov's dogs at school: conditioned to associate a bell with food, they slavered whenever it was rung. But the lesser-known fact, the teacher had said, was that when Pavlov's lab flooded, the dogs lost their conditioning. A trauma, a shock, a revolution—you can lose what you've learnt that way. Since the birth, you've forgotten all of your passwords. Your days feel like waking dreams. You don't know how to talk to people without being honest. You can't remember how to forget all of the things that have hurt you. You can't remember how to forget that all of the things that are supposed to be joyful have also hurt you.

The owl calls out again. Ola from downstairs told you, when you first moved in, that there was a pair of owls who visited the street, but you've never heard them before. The baby raises her small, fat hands in the air, twists her wrists and points her fingers as though she's conducting an orchestra in her sleep.

It's the caring that has been the trauma. It's the caring and the being cared for that has been the shock. After you gave birth, the midwife who was about to sew you up stroked your hand. *I'm going to be ever so careful, love*, she said. *Don't you worry, I do needlework at home*. And you felt, in that moment, like a precious, embroidered glove. Or you felt how it might feel to be a child with a mother who cares for her. It is the tenderness of the details that has broken you apart: the tiny scar at the baby's belly button, the tuft of hair at the nape of her neck, her tongue, Christ, the baby's tiny, perfect tongue, rough and clean as a kitten's. And that woman in white, it's the detail of her top riding up that you keep thinking of. You didn't even see her face, just her pale, naked torso, and the line of fabric that must have been her bra. Was there anyone else to care about these things? Are you the only mother of them?

The baby has settled to sleep in your arms. You look at her. At the feathered veins of her eyelids, finer than lines of purple silk. At the tiny creases in her lips. Have I not numbered each hair upon your head? Have I not picked off each flake of cradle cap, scooped out the soft wax from your new ears? You listen for the baby breathing. And when you cannot hear it, you pull her in closer and then you feel her breathe against your own chest. That tiny rasp is her inhale. You turn off the light from your phone. I heard you before you were born; I'll listen for you always in the dark. You reach one arm under the duvet, find Ali's warm belly, rising and falling. The night is an echo chamber. The owl is repeating itself outside. A lone woman, staggering down the ginnel, is deep in conversation with herself.

Your own mother is not so very far away. She's sleeping on a sofa in the den on Brownlow Street, half a mile off. And though you cannot know this yet, soon she'll hold your baby. You'll see her in the street. And you'll be afraid when she lifts the baby up. Her hands will be shaking, she'll smell like grass and smoke, she'll weep on the baby's head. And if you never see her again, you'll have this—this moment of her trembling care.

Forever chemicals

That summer, we spent each night knotted together in Nathan's single bed, beneath a blue Transformers duvet cover. We would wake at daybreak. We made jam sandwiches in the half-light of his mum's kitchen and then we'd cycle through the silent streets of the estate. We'd hit the main road of Peacehaven—a strip of pet shops, insurance brokers and funeral directors running parallel to the coast—and once we'd cycled across the street, the sea would be in sight. We'd follow the path down the back of the retirement bungalows, the flowers phosphorescent in the dawn light, the air scented with salt and pollen, and then we would be out there, right on the cliff edge. We'd throw our bikes and then our bodies down onto the grass. And we would watch the sun glitter immense and orange on the ocean. The light seemed to spread all the way from the beginning; from when the world was pristine.

I had known Nathan for almost a year by then. On my first day at sixth-form college, I caught the bus along the coast and Brighton had appeared in the window as a gorgeously decrepit apparition: buildings mouldered in the sea air; great regency facades concealed squats and chronic damp. I'd spent my childhood abroad. My father's work had taken us to the Hague and Hong Kong and, latterly, Zurich. I'd never had a friendship that had lasted for more than two years. Our belongings had been loaded into freight containers and we'd followed them once again—to a new house on a new estate at the edge of Peacehaven at the southern edge of England, where my father would retire. My new peers at the Brighton college were grungey and chaotic—they had lived twice the life that I had and spoke with thrilling openness about substance dependencies and heartbreak and self-harm and protest marches and other illicit forms of hope and desperation. Nathan and his friends took me in. They shared their drinks and their spliff and their beds, and they initiated me into long conversations over fires on the beach in which we talked about the peculiarities of our families, and music and films and books, and politics and universities and the future, and they asked me to tell them stories of faraway cities in which I had lived.

Every day, one of us would swim. The movement towards the sea was like surface tension breaking; all of us sitting there on the beach, talking and drinking, the energy building, until finally someone would break away—*Fuck it, I'm going in. Anyone coming?* Sometimes several of us would run down to the shore, throwing off our shoes on the way. Sometimes it would remain a solo mission, one head, dark as a seal's, out there on the horizon. The sea here was filthy, someone had told me. I know now that it was full of mercury and PCBs and dioxins and pesticides. But we swam in it anyway, choosing not to care—or perhaps, feeling our bodies to be inviolable. Sometimes we fished for mackerel, standing knee-deep at the shore while men off their heads on lager and ketamine pissed openly into the waves a few metres away from us. We cooked the fish over the fire, peeled away the blackened skin, and flaked the flesh from the bones with our fingers and teeth and tongues.

I moved between members of the group even-handedly at first, trying out different intimacies: late-night pashing with Mel, listening to poetry at Shabs's house at parties that her parents threw, going to gigs with Ike and his older brothers. Every few weeks the group would quietly re-tesselate, and someone else would be drawing-up close to me on the beach, sitting next to me to share their bottle of rum-laced ginger beer.

Just before our final exams, Nathan and I drew closer. I know the exact moment it happened. We were at a bus stop in Brighton. It was May, but the wind off the Channel was bitter. This was the first spring that I'd spent in England since being a small child.

Why is it still so cold? I said to Nathan as we waited together. I can't get used to it here. Doesn't it warm up even in spring?

Give here, Nathan said. And he took my hands and pushed them up inside his jumper, against the warm skin of his stomach. I laughed. The fuzz of his belly felt obscenely soft. Then he took one of my hands to his mouth, and pushed my fingers right in.

I was surprised and giddy and slightly weirded out. His hot mouth mollusced around my cold skin. The gesture seemed selfless and instinctive and too much.

The bus was pulling in. Nathan let my fingers go free and I wiped them on my coat, and then he looked ashamed.

Sorry, he said.

Don't be, I said.

*

All that summer then, it was me and Nathan and the ocean. I'd go back to the new house on Sundays to see my parents, but otherwise I stayed with Nathan. Each morning we made our pilgrimage to the water and swam. On the way back from the beach, Nathan would steal summer passionflowers from the front gardens of retirees and push them into my hair. He had a thing for flowers and plants. He told me that passionflowers were day bloomers, that they closed their petals at night, like dandelions and crocuses and African daises, responding to light and heat and the rhythms of the day. When we got back to his room, he would place the flowers carefully in a saucer of water on his bedside table, and as we chatted and ate crisps and watched films and fell asleep together, they would silently close. In the morning they would be revived—open and briefly beautiful again.

Nathan learned about plants from an old-timer at the care home where his mum worked. When he was younger, Nathan had spent evenings trailing his mum around Sunnyside as she served meals to men propped up in bed and washed their private parts. We traded tales of our childhoods. I told him how, in Zurich, on special occasions, we would melt cheese and add champagne to make fondue, and all of the food we ate would be covered in this rich, bland glue. I taught him to sing happy birthday in Dutch—*hieperdepiep!* He told me about the camaraderie and obscene humour at Sunnyside, that it smelt of sawdust and overripe bananas and that the men liked to give him small treats—pound coins, and copies of *Viz*, and bags of sherbet. Some of them told Nathan tremulous tales of long-ago love and filth.

I picked her up on the train the day I got out of prison... these stories would begin; or, *She was a big girl and she knew what to do...* Cedric was different. Cedric didn't just tell him tales: he taught him things. Cedric grew tomatoes and marigolds and nasturtiums in his room. Every surface was covered in them, making the place smell peppery and green. He showed Nathan how to pollinate flowers with a small brush to make the fruit come, and how to pinch out side-shoots to make a plant grow taller. Cedric had worked most of his life for the estate at Nymans. He'd looked after the tallest trees in Sussex—the coastal redwood—and he'd helped to replant them after the Great Storm. The rose gardens at Nymans had over a hundred varieties and Cedric had helped to cultivate unique hybrids there; Nymans established one of the first wild gardens way back when. Nathan could tell you anything you wanted to know about Nymans, and more.

If my exams went well, I was set to go to Leeds to study Law. Then I wanted to do an internship with an environmental charity. I was going to help change the world. I was going to help make the sea clean again. Nathan was going to try for a BTEC in Horticulture. He would stay in Sussex and study at Plumpton on an estate of a thousand acres and learn to tend to the soil and its inhabitants.

One evening in late August we lay together in his bed, watching the mackerel clouds through the skylight above us.

We can't just keep doing everything the same, can we? he said.

What do you mean? I said.

With you going away.

But that's ages away, I said.

Then I thought about it properly. The letters about my accommodation, the reading lists, the pans my mum had bought me—it was true that I would be starting university soon. I was so used to moving that I didn't register time or dwell on change in the way that most people do. I used to have a gift—or a pathology—for existing intensely in the present.

I didn't know, back then, that some things accumulate in the body forever: first love and polyfluoroalkyl substances.

We've got the rest of the summer together, I said. It's at least a fortnight.

A *fortnight*? he said. A *fortnight*? When were you going to tell me that? Fucking hell, Sylvie.

The next morning, the light at Nathan's thin blue curtains glowing as though it had never gone dark, the tone of Nathan's voice was different.

I think we should swim at the quarry this morning, he said.

Why? I asked. I twisted my limbs around his and thought of those trees he'd told me about that grow parasitically inside another.

Why not the sea?

It'll be warmer in the quarry, he said.

But the sea was warm enough yesterday, I said.

We should swim at the quarry, he said again, and he got up from the bed, shedding my limbs with ease.

The bike ride to the quarry was uphill and much longer than the one to the sea. I was lightheaded by the time we got there. The earth was chalky and coated my pumps. It had grown properly light, but the sky was dull. We sat down in the too-bright grey and ate our breakfast sandwiches.

When we'd finished, Nathan stood up and started taking off his clothes.

What are you doing? I asked. Why are you being like this?

I'm going for a swim, he said. His mouth was flat and hard. He wouldn't look at me. I'd never known him to be like this.

We were at the uppermost side of the quarry, a good twenty feet above the water—which was thickly green below us. It was impossible to tell how shallow the pool might be. Nathan had begun to stretch his arms out behind him.

You're not going to do it from here? Don't be a dickhead, I said. You know why they call it tombstoning?

He didn't reply.

Nathan pushed his shoulders back, and I heard the small bones at the top of his spine crack into place. He stretched his arms upwards. With the white cliffs of the quarry behind him, his body looked horribly fleshy. In one rush, he sprinted to the edge and hurled himself away from me.

♦

I fly over the North Atlantic twice a week for work. I fly over the Alboran Sea, over the Strait of Gibraltar, over the Canaries, down the west coast of Africa. From far above, the ocean only seems to travel in one direction. The waves crash towards the beach like the tumbling sheafs of collapsing buildings. The damage done to the ocean is mostly invisible. With an oil spill you can at least see it—the dirt and drama and pathos of it. But the damage from an oil spill is nothing in the grand scheme of destruction. Sometimes I see colourful patches below me in the sand—aquamarine and orange—which look cheerful from a holiday-maker's distance. But I know they'll be lines of fishing rope wrapped around the body of a porpoise or a seal. My job is to record what happens at sea and to collect evidence in the hope of future prosecutions. We record the industrial trawlers from the EU working illegally out here, dredging the ocean floor at night. We make notes on collateral damage—we estimate the mass of small fish and mammals and birds caught up in fishing nets and thrown back to rot. We base our estimates on what we can discover at ports and on whistle-blowers' reports. We monitor pollution and analyse the water. We measure the microplastics that fill the stomach of the sea, that degrade to produce massive dead zones where the water is a milky, toxic soup. We monitor the levels of forever chemicals, the per- and polyfluoroalkyl substances that stick to the kidneys of fish and mammals and accrete all the way up the food chain.

It's a long time since I've seen Nathan. Fifteen years, almost. When I left for university, he blanked my calls and my messages. He didn't respond to any of my letters. When I was back visiting, he never came out with the others. I was too proud to knock on his door, but still, for a long time, whenever I was very drunk, whenever I felt like I was falling into deep water, I'd call him. At first, I cried into his answerphone when I was homesick—a feeling I'd not known before, this longing for a place and for a person left behind. Later, I'd leave messages in which I sighed, longingly, intoxicatedly. Later still—when I was working and living in strange new cities and sleeping with strange new men—I'd leave long strings of obscene, confused invective in the middle of the night. I knew it was wrong, but I couldn't help it. His number was burned into my brain and

I kept coming back here, to that summer when we were together in the water.

I'm with Shabs at The Druids in Brighton when I finally see him again. It's sauna-hot in here and the atmosphere is one of libidinous holiday-making. I come back to England twice a year now to visit my parents, and to see the old crew. The pub is packed and when someone barges through, it feels like it could go either way. A flirtation or a fight. It always hits me when I'm back in an English seaside pub: the barely latent aggression of socialising here, the proximity of alcohol and naked skin and violence.

We're several drinks in when Shabs says: Oi. Look. Nathan's over there. Haven't seen him in proper ages.

Then she looks at me. Oh shit, she says. Sorry, Sylv.

It's alright, I say. It's not like you have to pretend he's dead.

But it doesn't feel alright. The floor is beginning to roil. I've a feeling in my stomach like seasickness.

Oh man, she says, I think he's coming over. Do you want me to—

Shabs! Nathan says, clamping a hand on her shoulder. What's up, mate?

Easy, easy, she says. Then she nods in my direction.

Alright, he says. Alright. I'm Nathan, Shabs's long-lost friend.

I know, I say.

As he looks at me properly, his face slackens. There's a resemblance to the Nathan I knew. The same squared-off stance—the defensive posture of a boy who wishes he was taller. The same glittering eyes. But there are differences too. His hair is almost entirely gone—it's shaved close now. His skin is tanned and oily and it crinkles when he smiles. When he doesn't, there's a new exhaustion. His cheeks pit inwards. His eyelids are purple.

He's recognised me.

Christ, he says. Sylvie?

Nathan and his friends buy us drinks. It's Nathan's first night out after the arrival of his second child, a baby girl they've named Lily. Nathan is married to a Pilates teacher called Willow and lives out in Shoreham. He works for the local council as a gardener. He looks after the park and the seafront planting. In the summer, he tells us, it's not so hard to manage a new baby: he naps under bushes on his lunch hour.

We all drink to wet the baby's head. Nathan stands so close that I can smell him—a time-warp mix of salt and sweetness.

Let's go for a swim, Shabs says when the bar rings closing time.

Nathan says he should be getting home, but the others jeer at him. Come on, mate, who knows when you're going to get let out again?

This ok with you? he asks.

Yes, I say. Yes, of course.

There's a certain point in summer on the south coast of England when, at night-time, the air and the water become the same temperature. It's dark on the beach, and I strip to my pants and don't give a shit about stones under foot. Nathan and I walk into the sea side-by-side, without touching. The others grow distant behind us.

Once we're submerged, the water and the sky are almost indistinguishable: the world around us is black and ambient.

We begin to swim, synchronised, out towards the end of the pier.

A little way out he calls to me: Wait up, Sylvie. We shouldn't go out any further.

I slow. I tread water and then turn around.

He's lying on his back. I turn over onto my back too and feel my hair unfurl around me. The sky is another sea, vast and studded with broken light. And here we are again, floating together in all this gunk.

Sounds from the beach reach us intermittently. Laughter. Shrieking. Music. Closer by there is the lulling shoosh of the waves, and the clink, a little way off, of floats fastened to the pier.

Something soft caresses me under the water. My skin prickles at the warm, alien contact and I kick myself upright and away from it.

When I was young and learning to swim in the sea off Lamma Island, I was afraid of things touching me under the water: a crab-claw or a tentacle or a jelly or the tip of something fiercer. The beaches round Hong Kong were circled with shark nets. Now, that fear seems quaint. Most of those animals are being disappeared. The endangered list includes sea turtles, balanea whales, blue whales, fin whales, sei whales, sea lions, bluefin tuna, Galápagos penguins. Finless sharks sink to the floor of the ocean. I've watched dolphins and porpoises turned to blooms of blood in the water. How quaint it was of me to fear that something *living* might be touching me.

Nathan is still floating on his back. I've practised this conversation with him in my head so many times. I have to ask him now or I never will.

Why did you ghost me, Nathan? I say.

Nathan splashes upright now too.

Ghost you? *Mate*, he says. Let's not do this.

His features are in darkness. The outline of his head is buoyish.

Then he says: Look, you were never going to stay round here, were you? You're only back on holiday now, aren't you? I was doing you a favour. And what did I get for it? Years of you hating me. All those fucking messages, telling me what a shit I was. Nah, Sylvie, I'm not having it.

I have a truly awful thought then. We're back at the quarry on that humid grey morning. And I imagine Nathan diving over that edge again, only this time I picture him hitting something below, something hard and fatal. I'm imagining that he tombstoned properly.

Look, I'm sorry if that was... harsh, he says. I didn't mean... I didn't want to... Sorry, yeah? But look, I need to get back. We should swim back in.

You go, I say. I'm going to stay out here for a bit.

You sure? he says.

Yeah, I say. I want to swim for a bit longer. I'm alright out here. You don't need to worry.

Okay, he says. If you're sure. Don't get cold though, yeah? I'm glad... I'm glad I saw you again, Sylvie. You look like you're doing well.

He turns away from me and starts to swim towards the shore. There are glimmering lights all along the front and small fires illuminating the shingle. The pier is in darkness—shut down for the night. When I look for Nathan again, I can't see him. There is only the broken, glittering surface of the water. The plash plashing of the waves against the pier's stilts.

I make myself unmurder him in my head. I imagine us back on the quarry edge and this time Nathan doesn't jump in the water at all. He doesn't leap away from me. Instead he lies down next to me. We wrap around each other. Our bodies are chalk and grass and young and clean.

I turn onto my back in the water, and then I feel that anonymous touch again. Ribbons of softness gliding through the water column, trailing past and underneath me. I let them move against me without recoiling. I let them ghost themselves against my belly and down the inside edge of my thigh. This could be an ocean phantom—a plastic bag or a broken fishing net. Whatever's left of an animal tossed back to sea. But couldn't it be something living, still? The tentacles of a sea jelly. A moon fish or a compass jellyfish. Seahorse. Cuckoo wrasse. Cat shark. Sunfish. A shoal of mackerel—their bodies so exquisitely sensitive that a thousand fish move towards the deep as one.

Animals at night

The car window frames the view like a postcard: the long lawn, the slanting apple tree, the sheer blue sky rising above the cottage's slate roof. Totally lush. Ayesha sits in the back seat of the hire car. No desire to move and imprint herself on this pristine picture. For a moment, there is only this—this scene of possible future enjoyment. There's nothing she has to do, nothing that the baby needs, nothing to worry about.

Looks nice, Tom says. Good job, Ayesh.

Ayesha has done all of the work for this trip. She found the cottage online. She coordinated dates for everyone. She booked the hire car and packed everything they could possibly need. This is their first proper trip since Sofia was born—and the first time they'll see Hanna and Piers since both babies arrived, within a fortnight of one another, the winter before last. Hanna's baby had been due at Christmas and was finally coaxed into the world on New Year's Eve with fireworks and Syntocinon; baby Sofia had come early, hurtling into the cold, grey blear of early January in a hospital corridor.

Are we going in then or what? says Tom.

Ayesha opens the car door. Heads round to unstrap baby Sofia, who will need feeding soon. There's a noise under foot as she moves. A rasp. Stones. Christ. Stones everywhere. The lower portion of the garden, this parking area, is composed of small stones. The pathway that they are now following up to the cottage door is formed of these same stones. Stones that baby Sofia will immediately try to eat. Round, glossy lozenges just the right size to block the baby's epiglottis.

Scrunch of tyres. Another car swings into the parking area, a large, supple shark of a vehicle, with Piers behind the wheel. Ayesha waves. Piers doesn't respond. Ayesha and Tom walk back down the pathway together and wave again. Ayesha even persuades baby Sofia to wave her little hand. But Piers and Hanna are deep into something.

Hanna throws her hands up and gets out of the passenger side. Clocks the three of them and grins.

Fucking hell, Hanna says, what a journey.

Hanna is in loose, black clothes and clutches a slim, gold phone in one hand, white knuckled. She looks thinner than when they all last met. Which was when, exactly? Ages ago. Two years, thereabouts. They'd met for summer drinks in a beer garden in Islington, Ayesha and Hanna both queasy and disoriented by early pregnancy. This is the longest they've gone since university without seeing each other.

He's only just gone to sleep, Hanna says, cocking her head towards the car. He screamed the whole way round the M25.

Tom lumbers round to Hanna to give her a bear hug.

Careful, big man, Hanna says.

Tom moves differently around Hanna—chest barrelled out, four-pints-down swagger. How had Ayesha forgotten this?

Ayesha follows Tom, leans in to kiss Hanna, holds Sofia round towards her like an offering.

Oh my, Hanna says. She strokes a fingertip lightly down baby Sofia's cheek. What a love! She's still so wee. Just wait until Theo wakes up. He's a beast.

Piers is out of the car now too. His hair pushed behind his ears, his eyes heavy, his skin deeply tanned. Over the last decade, they've mostly met up for festivals and parties and after-parties. Piers has looked this gorgeously destroyed forever.

Have you got the cool box? Hanna says, already walking away from him. This place looks perfect. Let's go and get shitfaced.

The cottage is small but well-equipped. There's an open-plan living area and two en suite bedrooms. There is a basket of local produce and a bottle of champagne on the countertop. Ayesha sets baby Sofia down to toddle, but almost immediately Sofia slips hard. The flooring throughout the cottage comprises large, polished tiles. Sofia's hands make a sharp slapping sound against the hard surface. Why didn't she spot this on the pictures, or the stones outside? Ayesha will have to watch Sofia constantly, inside and out, for the whole weekend.

Aw, says Hanna, laughing. Poor little wobbler.

Hanna is rooting through the cupboards, looking for champagne flutes.

We'll have to use these, she says, gathering up a clutch of large wine glasses. Let's go outside so we can leave Theo in the car till he wakes.

In the garden there's a wooden table, faded to grey and barnacled with fungus. They wipe down the chairs, pick off blobs of bird shit using baby wipes.

Thanks for finding this place, Ayesh, Piers says. It's been too long. We've really missed you guys.

Yes, ta very much for sorting it, says Hanna. I'd have never gotten round to it. Things are just insane at work.

Hanna works at a law firm in the City. She looks after copyright, but it's still music-related—she's still looking after musicians, just at the meta level now, she always says. Hanna doesn't gig any more, but she tells scandalous stories about badly behaved minor musicians propositioning her and passing out in her office after accusing people of stealing their tunes. Ayesha half-listens to her current story about a terrible new partner and the hours she's being forced to work, but she is also watching Tom walking Sofia across the lawn. He's holding Sofia's arms above her head in just the way that she's asked him not to—it makes it even harder for her to learn to balance on her own.

Hanna pops the bottle open, pours yellow fizzy wine approximately across four glasses.

Oh, I won't actually, Han—

What! We're on holiday aren't we? Even if it is only for a night. Ayesha, duck, don't tell me we're not allowed any fun at all now? She pouts. She's gone proper Manc.

I'll save it for later, Ayesha says. I'm still... feeding Sofia, so I'm trying to be a bit careful.

Christ, says Hanna. You've got to be able to have something for yourself. Seriously, love, at this point? Sixteen months deep?

Ayesha can see out of the corner of her eye that Sofia's cheek is distended. There's something in there, secreted in the pouch of her mouth.

Ayesha stands up.

Tom, check her mouth! she shouts. Then she's running.

Tom swings Sofia up into the air, mimes a big open O. Baby Sofia's lips stay clamped shut.

Ayesha hooks her finger into Sofia's hot mouth, emptying it of two small stones.

They're everywhere, Tom. You've got to watch her all the time. You can't take your eyes off her, not even for a moment.

Fuck's sake, he says under his breath. I'm doing my best. You watch her then.

Ayesha walks with Sofia around the perimeter of the garden, at a distance from the conversation. Hanna is describing their nanny, an older woman who appears at their house at 6 a.m. each morning and reprimands Hanna for working too hard. Ayesha watches Hanna tilt her long white neck back to gulp the champagne. She watches Tom wipe his mouth with the back of his hand. She searches the grass for tiny pebbles and throws them hard into the flower beds.

A high-pitched sound sirens in towards them.

Piers is jog-running down the lawn past Ayesha towards the cars. Of course: baby Theo. His cry is so different from Sofia's—so much louder, with such mechanical force.

Piers unstraps Theo from the car, performs some brief ritual of pacification, brings him up the garden towards Ayesha and Sofia.

Ayesha lifts Sofia up to greet him. Hello, baby Theo, she says, waving Sofia's hand.

His eyes are still full of tears.

We've messed up his sleep routine, says Piers. Poor little fellah doesn't know what's going on. He snuzzles his face into Theo's fat cheek.

The baby is big and tan and dimpled, with thick blond hair.

He's gorgeous, Ayesha says. He looks like you, and like Hanna too.

He's a little beauty, Piers says. I just hope he gets Hanna's looks... and her brains as well.

Pretty boy, they used to call Piers at uni, or, more meanly, Piers-nice-but-dim. But he wasn't dim. Isn't. He's softly spoken and too conciliatory—affable to a fault. Hanna didn't used to let him speak when they went to pubs outside of Fallowfield or on any occasion that they'd tried to score drugs. *You're a liability,* Hanna would say. *You keep your vowels to yourself.*

Things must be difficult for you guys, Ayesha says. With Hanna's hours.

Oh, it's not so bad, he says. You know me, I've always kept strange hours. I do the night-times, so that Han isn't too knackered for work. Then I do a bit of pottering in the day.

Piers occasionally reviews albums for one of the big London papers, but Ayesha can't now remember which one. Mostly he writes copy for specialist magazines—*Angler's World, Cycling Today, The Modern Bride*—while he works on a novel about the music world that never seems to get any closer to completion.

Anyway, it can't be easy for you guys, he says. With Tom gigging, and you back at work. Must help being close to your family though?

Sort of, Ayesha says.

A year before Sofia was born, Ayesha and Tom made the move from London back to the North. She'd decided to go legit, to get a proper teaching qualification and a job in a school. No more weekend wedding gigs, no more evenings sitting in north London living rooms, trying to make indifferent kids play scales on expensive pianos. Her teaching salary meant they'd been able to buy a terraced house in Sowerby Bridge—a picturesque town if you looked down the valley towards Hebden Bridge, rather than up its steep walls to the council blocks and sedimented poverty. Ayesha's mother now came round once a week, mostly to diagnose Sofia's potential health and developmental problems. No one visited in the evenings; no one had come in those long nights early on when Tom was gigging in Manchester and she'd walked Sofia—screaming, teething, feverish, desperate to be held but wild even in her arms—around the small living room while the neighbours hammered on the wall. *You should have lived closer by*, her mother often says. *Nice houses on our street, bigger than this one. What's wrong with Halifax now?*

Knock, knock! A white woman in a windcheater is standing in the parking area, miming knocking on an imaginary door. Oh, you must be Ayesha. Of course. Of course. You got in ok then? I'm Margaret.

Hi, Ayesha says. Yes, the keys were just where you said.

Good. Good. Would the children like to come and feed the hens?

For lunch, they go to a pub, the only pub near the cottage, and they sit around another picnic table in the weak sunshine. It's just the six of them in the beer garden. A blackbird is busy in the hedge to one side of them. Theo is asleep again in his pram. Hanna cuts her steak with a serrated knife and the thin red blood pools on her plate. Ayesha has to sit sidesaddle at the table. Sofia is in the sling in front of her.

Theo loved it, Piers says. I don't think he's seen hens before, has he Han? They were both having a good little toddle around.

Until she just drops the *Cam-pylo-bacter* bomb, right, Ayesh? *Just make sure they wash their hands thoroughly*, she says. *You don't want them contracting campylobacter.*

Yeah, that's a nasty bacteria, Tom says. Tom is the only one of them who grew up rural.

Yeah, says Piers. Well, I know that now. Googled it straight away. Guys, have you started to worry about weird things? Like, obsessively? Something funny has happened to my brain since Theo was born. Piers is eating chips as he speaks, taking several at once and jamming them into ketchup, then pushing them into his mouth. Like, near-misses? Sometimes I can't stop thinking about them, playing stuff out in my head over and over.

I know what you mean, Ayesha says. I sometimes get the same. It's always me though, doing something awful. Like dropping Sofia. Or just watching her slip under the bath water. Or letting her pram go right in front of a car.

Piers stops shovelling chips.

Shit, Ayesh, that's horrible, Piers says. He's looking at her with concern.

Ayesha, Hanna says, how much sleep are you getting? Tom, are you actually doing anything at night? Does Sofia always sleep in the sling like that, right on top of you? You must be totally knackered if you don't even get a break when she sleeps. You might be anaemic if you're still not eating meat, you know, Ayesh, and that messes with your head. I had to take a whole lot of iron after the birth. I'd lost so much blood. Honestly, at this point, it's me or the steak.

Hanna turns the point of her knife towards Tom.

Look after baby Ayesha, please. Can't you make yourself useful and at least cut up her pizza?

Tom puts his arms around Ayesha. Kisses her on the top of the head.

Ayesh is a total trooper, he says.

Ayesha has planned a walk for them for the afternoon. It had looked straight forward when she found the route on her phone, but now the signal is patchy and she can't locate them on the map. They're on the main road, and now, surely, they just need to follow it for a bit, until the turn-off. It should be less than two miles.

But there's another problem: up ahead of them, the footpath peters out, leaving just the road. It's as though pedestrians are meant to vaporise at this point on the A606.

Hanna and Piers are arguing about how to proceed.

You can't just push him on the road, Hanna says, into oncoming traffic.

But that's exactly what you're meant to do, Piers says. Face the oncoming traffic. That's the highway code.

Not with a fucking pushchair, she says. There are lorries along this road.

Where the pavement runs out, there is a narrow grassy embankment.

Could we walk on the grass? Ayesha says. She's still carrying Sofia in the sling. She steps up onto the banking. It's uneven, but passable.

We need to go back and get the cars, Hanna says.

Let me try the pushchair up there, says Piers. He rams their Maclaren at the verge. The ground is too uneven for him to continue.

You'll break it, Hanna says. Just fucking stop. This is impossible.

I'll carry the pushchair, Tom says. And you can carry Theo, mate. It's not far, right, Ayesh?

Shouldn't be, she says.

They walk along in convoy: Tom at the front, carrying the pushchair; Piers carrying baby Theo; Ayesha carrying baby Sofia; Hanna at the rear, carrying both change bags.

After a while, Hanna stops and dumps the bags on the ground. This is ridiculous, she shouts down the line. How much further is it?

They all check their phones again: no reception, their map apps are unpeopled.

I'll run ahead, Tom says. See if I can spot the turning.

You're a hero, mate, Piers says.

Ayesha mooshes her lips in Sofia's hair. Piers bounces around with Theo. Two lorries rattle past in quick succession and drown out all other sound.

When Tom appears again, he's breathless. He bends over for a moment, his hands on his knees, then stands and says: It's only just around the corner. There's a pavement on the other side up ahead and signs for the reserve.

Good job, big man, Hanna calls from the back as they set off again.

Oh, Tom calls over his shoulder back down the line, there's something pretty nasty up ahead. An animal. Dead. You might not want Theo to see it. I'll tell you when we're close.

What is it? Ayesha shouts back up the line. Roadkill?

Not sure, Tom says. It's a hare, I think. Don't look at it, guys. It's grim.

As they approach a small dip in the embankment, Tom gestures over towards a scrub of nettles near the hawthorn that edges the grass. It's just up there, he says. So look at the road or something.

Ayesha holds Sofia's body through the cloth of the sling, gathering her weight into her arms. She kisses the top of her head ferociously. Piers is bouncing Theo again, and pointing to things in the sky to make sure his gaze is away from the ground.

As she moves past the nettles, Ayesha glances down. It's impossible not to. It's like when someone tells you not to look at the sun, and then of course you're drawn towards its blinding glare. At first, Ayesha can only see green. And then, amongst the dark serrations of the nettle leaves, her eyes find a brighter, more lucent pool of colour. The animal's fur is fawn and brown, its paws disappear into the undergrowth. But its face, or what is left of its face, is indelibly visible: the thin ears flattened back in fear; the elongated snout; its small throat covered with black-red blood, still wet. Its face is raw and entirely skinless.

They turn off the main road and into an industrial estate. Theo is back in his pram, and the walking is easier. The entrance to the reserve is an additional mile through the estate, which wasn't clear on the route Ayesha had seen. They pass a small manufacturing plant, and several anonymous, white buildings, and a commercial bakery—all of them deserted.

Please. Stop. Fricking. Talking about it, Hanna says.

They've been speculating about the hare. Each of them, it turns out, had been unable not to look. Tom thinks it must have been attacked by something, that a predator must have eaten part of the hare's face before being disturbed. But Piers remembers reading a news story recently about myxomatosis, about how it's spreading again. Maybe it's passed to hares now?

Maybe, says Tom. Ulceration can get pretty nasty. It can sometimes look like the flesh has been eaten.

But, on balance, Tom thinks it unlikely. Hares are actually closer to deer than rabbits, you know, he says. Totally different species. Can it even pass to them?

That's the thing, Piers says. We can't predict how these kinds of diseases spread, can we? We introduced it in Europe, right? To control the wild rabbit population? And then it spreads to domestic rabbits, then who knows what else?

What did I say? Hanna says. Shut up. Please shut the fuck up. This is meant to be a holiday.

Piers tries to start a new conversation.

You know, if you found yourself in a survival situation in the English wilds and you hunted rabbits, you'd actually waste away, no matter how much you ate, because of the high protein content. It's called rabbit starvation.

You google too much, mate, Tom says.

They walk in silence until they hit the car park for the nature reserve, which is deserted too. They open a gate onto a field that has been left to go wild. In the far corner is a small play area.

Is this it? Hanna says. Is this the nature reserve?

I guess so, says Ayesha.

The field is mashed up—great tractor treads criss-cross in the mud—and a fine cloud of wild flowers hazes above the churned-up earth. Dots of magenta and violet and cornflower-blue. Theo and Sofia toddle happily through the long stems, shrieking at bees and hoverflies. The scent from the earth is heady and violently fresh. It makes Ayesha slightly dizzy, this strong, skunky green. Oh man, it's wild to be outside. And to see the two of them like this: Sofia and Theo, little burbling creatures in the grass. Sofia walking in a meadow. Makes Ayesha tender and also sad. Such a strange, happy sorrow, when she sees Sofia do something new like this. The first time that will never again be a first time. And then you think: How many? How many meadows in a life? Whatever the number, it is finite. And never new again. Every new joy unhinged with grief like this.

When they reach the small playground, Tom and Piers lift the babies onto the old equipment. The swings are rusted. The roundabout groans as Piers pushes it.

Christ, Hanna says. This whole place is a tetanus trap. She laughs and turns to Ayesha. They are leaning together against the fencing at the edge of the tarmac. How are you, Ayesh? she says. I mean, *really*?

I'm okay, Ayesha says. I'm tired. But I'm okay, I think.

Are you though, love? Hanna says. Because you don't seem... yourself. You're sort of... distant. Hanna looks towards Theo. It's the hardest thing I've ever done. I don't mind saying that. The early days were awful. The feeding, Christ, that endless feeding, when you can't do anything else, and they're crying and crying, and you can't tell what's wrong with them. It sent me nuts.

A hundred days of darkness, Ayesha says. That's what someone told me. A hundred days of darkness, and then it's supposed to lift.

Ayesha's mother and her sister and her aunt had fed her through those days. Difficult as she'd found returning to proximity with her extended family, they'd known what to do in those first few weeks. They'd let themselves in to clean her house, left food in her fridge, and expected nothing from her in return—especially not happiness.

I'm sorry it got so bad, Han. I wish I'd known, Ayesha says.

Well, you were in the... acute phase too. I'm out of it now, thank fuck. But I think you're still there, Ayesh. You're... I don't know. Distracted the whole time. And Tom says... Look, even now, you can't take your eyes off Sofia. Tom's got her. She's fine. Ayesha, are you in there?

Hanna waves her hand in Ayesha's face.

It's true. She is distracted. She's watching Sofia on the swing. She's too small for it. If Tom pushes any harder, will she tip out?

You must be totally drained, Hanna says. Feeding her for this long. If it's too much, you should talk to your doctor, you know. I started some meds, and they're bloody marvellous. There's no shame in it, in asking for help. You don't have to be a martyr, Ayesh. Didn't we always say that we didn't have to do it their way? Like our mothers? That it didn't have to mean the end of our lives?

Hanna is waiting for a reply. Sofia is screaming in the swing. What can Ayesha say? That she feels, in every wonderful moment, that they are teetering on the brink of something terrible. That the way she loves Sofia is a kind of catastrophe. Does that mean that something is wrong with her? That she's being a martyr? Who knows how any of this is supposed to feel?

Sofia is still wailing in the swing.

I'm glad you're feeling better, Han, Ayesha says. I'm just going to sort out Sofia.

*

Hanna asks Piers to go back and get the car to drive them back to the cottage.

But isn't this the whole point of being out in the countryside? Piers says. To spend time in the fresh air?

The afternoon is turning golden. Piers insists they walk back.

So here they are again, marching in line along the grass embankment.

It's crazy, isn't it? Piers is shouting. We live in a totally different world from when these two were conceived.

Yeah, says Tom. What have we done to the poor little buggers? But even with all this shit, I wouldn't take it back.

Me neither, mate, says Piers. Not for anything. He's the best thing that's ever happened to me. He makes a raspberry on baby Theo's fat cheek.

It's coming up again, Tom shouts. The hare, in that patch over there. Honestly, guys, just look away this time.

They file past: Tom, Piers and baby Theo, Hanna, then Ayesha and baby Sofia. Ayesha tries—she really does try not to look. But her eyes flicker towards it at the very last moment.

And her gaze is caught, then, on something awful.

Stop, Ayesha shouts. Stop guys! Stop!

The line comes to a disorderly halt.

What's wrong? Tom puts down Theo's pushchair and turns towards Ayesha.

The hare, Ayesha says. I saw… something.

What she saw, when she glanced back towards the animal's skinless face, was movement: a twitch through its body.

I don't think it's dead, she says.

Why did you look? I told you... Guys, you stay there, Tom says. I'll have a gander.

Tom approaches the patch of nettles carefully. He pushes his hands up inside his jacket-sleeves to protect them, then parts the leaves. He watches in silence for a while. Then shakes his head. Shit, he says. I think you're right.

It can't be alive, Hanna says. Its face is...

Oh, God, says Piers. This is awful. What should we do?

What should we *do*? Hanna says. There's nothing we can *do*.

But it must be in agony, Piers says. What do you think, Tom?

Fucking hell, says Tom. I don't know. Its back leg's twitching. Maybe it's death throes or something?

We should kill it, Ayesha says.

Hanna whistles a long falling note.

Piers is moving from one foot to the other, jiggling as though he is trying to settle Theo, though Theo is entirely still and is watching Piers's face carefully.

What do you think, Tom? Piers says. You must have dealt with lots of sick animals.

Tom shrugs. What, cos I grew up on a farm?

Ayesha knows that Tom is terrified of death, close-up. He told her that the pigs cried like children when they were loaded for slaughter, and that he always wept when they were taken away. He left the farm as soon as he could.

We need to find something to finish it off with, Ayesha says. A heavy object, maybe. Or one of us could stamp on it?

Stamp on it? Ayesha, have you actually gone insane? Hanna says. We don't even know what's wrong with it. If it's got a disease and Tom gets covered in blood, he could pass something on to us. Or to the babies.

Why is it *me* who's covered in blood? says Tom.

Piers's face is pitiful. He makes a final appeal to Tom. Well, he says. If it's in its death throes, maybe we should leave it alone?

Yeah, I reckon, Tom says. It's definitely on its way out.

He's looking down at the ground now, away from Ayesha. He's grinding the toe of his shoe into a small clod of earth.

We should get Sofia and Theo away from it, he says.

You heard him, Hanna says. Don't give me that look, Ayesha. It's an animal. I don't see you sweep the grass before you walk on it. Why are we even still here?

Hanna turns and begins walking away down the embankment. Piers, she calls, bring Theo down this way.

Piers shrugs, then turns to follow Hanna.

We can't just leave it, Ayesha says. But Hanna and Piers are already synchronised and moving away.

Tom, she says, we should do something.

Tom's big, generous mouth is pulled in tight. It's as good as dead, Ayesh, he says. There's nothing we can do. Let's get Sofia away.

While Piers puts Theo to bed, Hanna mixes them all a drink in the kitchen. Ayesha senses Sofia softening towards sleep: kittenish, she curls up close to Ayesha on the sofa, trying to put her face into Ayesha's breasts. Ayesha scoops her into her lap.

Hanna dishes out the glasses. Nostrovia! she says. To your good health. And she knocks her drink back.

Christ, Tom says. This is strong. But fucking delicious. Thanks, Han. To old friends.

Ayesha sips from her glass. She's barely touched alcohol in the last two years. The drink makes her lips ring.

How's Sofia at bedtime then? Hanna asks.

She's an absolute nightmare, Tom says. Won't sleep for longer than about twenty minutes unless Ayesha's there right beside her.

You've got to knock that on the head, says Hanna. When I went back to work, Piers started doing bedtimes. Theo wailed for about a week, but now he sleeps like a dream.

Well, Tom's gigging most evenings, Ayesha says. And it's such a short time, really, isn't it, that they're this small? I miss her when I'm at work, so I'm just trying to make the most of our time together at night.

Hanna clenches her jaw and her cheeks flex inwards. Well, if I'm sleep-deprived, she says, I can't do my job. If I mess up, if I make even a little mistake, I can be sued, and then where would we be? Piers is making fuck all. We don't all have that option.

Oh, Ayesha says. I didn't mean anything...

But Hanna is already up and into the kitchen, banging about in the cupboards.

I'm going to make another round, she says. Where's that knife gone. She fumbles with a lemon on the countertop, her back turned to them. Ow! She sucks her finger.

Han, Tom is up now. Take it easy, mate. Don't get agitated.

Hanna turns towards him. Her eyes are bright and her hands are balled up. Tom steps in close to her. Relax, Han, he says. No one's having a go.

And then she puts her arms around his neck. Sorry, Ayesh, she says. She kisses Tom on the cheek. There's a lot resting on me just now. I'm wound up all the time. Sorry, Ayesh. Ignore me.

*

Ayesha lies in the bedroom listening to the others. This is how it often feels now: a distance between her and even her closest friends as they sail along their own separate courses. Theo went down easily, and now the others have music on low in the living room—someone new that Piers has discovered. They're getting drunk and reminiscing about their old lives, about gigs and parties and festivals on faraway beaches where they'd danced and played like animals at night, nocturnal and wild.

She's tried to settle Sofia, to leave her in the bedroom, but each time Ayesha moves, Sofia yawps awake.

I'm sorry, Ayesh, Tom whispered a few minutes ago, head through the door. Can I do anything?

No, she'd said. It's fine. I'll lie with her until she's deeper under.

Sorry you're missing out, he said. We've got a drink waiting for you.

She hadn't replied.

Sofia is still latched on. She's curled into Ayesha's body like a comma. These nights settling Sofia, which at first had seemed so hard, so impossibly long—why oh why would a creature need to feed so much, how could a creature be so raw and needful?—these long nights are now her deepest pleasure. A decade ago, it had been her nights with Tom that brought her joy. When they were still at university and he'd been jilted by Hanna, she had comforted him, taken him to her bed, and their bodies had made so much pleasure, and they'd moved together through the night-times, dancing and drinking and laughing and making more and more pleasure.

Now, there's this new nocturnal intimacy. Totally illegible. No one talks to her about night-time feeding. People ignore it, or pity her it, or attempt to counsel her out of it. Sofia will never remember these long nights. But here it is: this keen, vital pleasure between them. This animal heat of feeding an infant—Sofia's hot mouth filled with milk the same temperature as Ayesha's blood. Ayesha's nose in Sofia's hair, her scalp smelling of warm yeast and honey. Sofia curling into her, her tongue scalloping to make the milk come faster.

An image flashes into vividness in the dark: the raw face of the hare out there at the side of the road. Its flesh cooling in the night.

How long will it take for the creature to die? Hours? Days?

When she'd birthed Sofia, Ayesha had felt raw. Her wounds stung in air and water. She cried when anyone spoke to her kindly. She'd felt like an especially soft, fleshy animal, like an anemone or jellyfish, laid out and salted. And hadn't Sofia seemed raw too? That little purple lozenge of a body, early born. After the birth, for days, there'd been the rich, sweet smell of Ayesha's blood still coming away. And she'd missed it when the bleeding had finally stopped—when the bright violence of new life was folded back away again inside her. Never new again. All of these illegible moments of pleasure and grief.

A shaft of light. Tom is at the door again.

Ayesha, love, he says. I think Sofia's asleep. Why don't you come out? And if she wakes again, I can walk her outside.

He sits down next to her on the bed.

We shouldn't have left it there, she says, alone like that.

What? he says. What? Do you mean the hare? You're still thinking about that?

Silence. Hanna laughing at something in the living room.

I'll come in soon, Ayesha says. You go back to the others.

She closes her eyes. Maybe she can sleep for just a moment. A disco nap—like when her and Han used to curl up next to each other before a big night out. But there it is again: the thought of the animal, alone, barely a mile across the fields from here. They'd done nothing. Not one of them. They'd all of them been cowards. A memory of a long time ago: the four of them camping together in a yurt at the foot of the Black Mountains. Dancing in the rain at a micro-festival. Never properly dry or warm. Her and Han squatting in the long grass at the bottom of the field to piss together. Breakfast was served in a barn on the campsite, and one morning a bird had gotten caught inside. It had flown around and around, and then darted towards a low window. Hit it hard. Hit it three times, and then it lay stunned on the floor. No one had done anything. They had all just stared at it. And then Ayesha had gone to scoop it up in her hands, felt it quickening there like a heartbeat, released it back into the big rain-dark sky. Some people in the barn had clapped. She'd watched it fly for a minute or so, and then it had dropped straight down into the field.

When she leaves the bedroom, the others are cutting lines on the living-room table. They call after her:

Ayesh? Ayesha! Where are you going?

I can walk her if she won't settle. Ayesh, come and have some fun.

It's okay, she calls back to them. I won't be long.

They do not try to follow her.

Ayesha walks out into the dark garden. Sofia is strapped to her chest. When she gets to the end of the stone pathway, the voices of the others are far away from her and Sofia. She follows the driveway out to the road. She moves slowly, using the hedge to guide her. Her eyes are still adjusting. Out on the pavement, she picks up her pace. Sofia stares up at her in wonder. The lights are on in the pub and in some of the cottages. The night air feels cool, bitter, alien. Her lips taste of salt and liquor. She walks faster.

The smell of the main road—petrol and mown grass—hits as she turns onto it. It is quiet, at first, as she walks towards the embankment. There are no lights out here, but the sky is clear. She hears the lorry coming long before it appears. When it rounds the bend, the noise fills the night and its lights stun her. She is perfectly still. Sofia too. Eyes oily black and reflective. Once the lorry has passed, she waits for her vision to readjust, blinks out the light, then walks on. She is up on the embankment now. She trains her eyes on the foliage, searching for blood. She will use the light from her phone to find it. And then she will use her feet. She will not turn back until it is done.

Plausible objects

So we went up to Shell's and the dogs were going mad. She walks them infrequently, at the dead of night. *They're on that banned list now*, Shell told us once. *If anyone sees us, the police might come and confiscate them.* Trixie, an American Pit Bull, pinned me to the sofa and breathed meaty halitosis in my face. I could feel dog-spittle aerosoled all over my Christmas Day make-up.

She *probably* won't hurt you, Shell said.

Shell wasn't in the mood to cook, so we ate mince pies out of their little tinfoil dishes and necked vodka. Wardy told me that later on he was going to *make love to me*. He'd never used that expression before, so I was already unnerved.

It turned out he'd arranged for us to use his friend Siobhan's bedroom while she watched the *Doctor Who* Christmas special, because she'd done it out like a magical winter grotto—whited the windows with snow-spray, spangled stars everywhere, fixed a cascading fairy-tale-princess canopy over the bed. Just as he was due to make love to me, Wardy got his leg tangled up in the netting and pulled the whole glittering affair down on top of us. A bracket collided with my face and I started pissing blood from my nose all over Siobhan's powder-blue satin bedding.

Then we were in A&E. My Uncle David sat two rows behind us, coughing up bits of his tumour again. And it turned out the nurse who sewed up my nose had been on a blind date with Wardy just a few months before. She didn't make a very good job of my stitches.

We got out in the early hours of Boxing Day and tiny snowflakes bit at our faces through the dark. I made lists of plausible objects in my head. Wardy never tried to make love at me again.

Tell me what you like

She crosses the border into Northumberland in the dark and at speed. When she first set out, the sky had been milky over the Humber—the same cold colour it had been all winter. As she drove further north, the grey wash hardened and clarified. In her wing mirror, stratified cloud and ribbons of black. The sunset, when it came, had been imperceptible, the light simply going out. Even the dog had gone quiet.

People had told her that it was too soon for her to make the journey. Ewen had wanted to come up and meet her here. But she had been resolute. She'd packed the car quickly that afternoon, stowed the dog in the passenger seat, and, once rush hour had passed, she'd started on the length of the A1.

She hates driving alone at night. The streetlamps disappear up here, leaving only the cats' eyes to guide her through the blackness, and even though she knows the road well, it is newly unpredictable—the camber altering without warning, the glint of a real animal's eyes picked up in the foliage making the road momentarily seem to veer. And there are the other night-drivers too: erratic and aggressive cars on her tail or overtaking her, the drivers psychopathic blanks behind their headlights.

And she loves driving alone at night. When all other light is gone, she speeds up. The horizon here is long and low.

She turns a bend and suddenly the moon appears, spilling its light across black fields. She knows it's a sin against the environment to love to drive. But she's never had the courage to go out running at night and accelerating like this through the landscape is when she gets to feel most animal.

She leaves the car running while she unlocks the cottage. The car's headlamps are the only way to see before she sorts things inside. She'll find her way to the electricity meter with the light from her phone. When she unlocks the screen, she sees Ewen has left several messages. She'll leave off reading them until the morning. She feeds the meter, then flicks the hall light switch. She brings in two bags of groceries from the car. She plugs in the fridge. She carries her case up to the bedroom, and the dog follows, his claws clacking up the steep wooden staircase. He's old too. His straw-coloured hair has always looked parched, but now he's grey around his muzzle as well. She strips to her underwear. The bedsheets are so cold they feel damp. But she is too tired now to properly think or feel. She curls up with the dog and turns herself out like a light.

She wakes to the sound of the sea.

She has always loved coming up to this cottage. She bought it for a song more than forty years ago. A car of her own and a cottage by the sea; the two things that she'd most wanted, the two things that had seemed like the ultimate achievements of a life. She'd had childhood holidays here in Northumberland, and when she married Greg they had honeymooned here. The wind had been relentless, but, at the first sign of the afternoon sky softening, they had raced onto the beach to put up the windbreaker. They drove its wooden poles into the sand and it had stood skew-whiff, flinching brightly against the blast. There had been so much to say, to shout into the roar of wind and sea. She had laced the dune grass through her fingers, her new ring gleaming against the dull gold of the sand. After Ewen was born, they'd marked each holiday with the long drive up here. She'd washed Ewen's sandy, toddling feet in the cold tin bath and, when he was old enough, Greg had taught him how to build a real fire in the open grate. She had often watched the two of them working together, constructing lattices of wood, as she folded strips of newspaper to make firelighters.

And she had dreaded coming to the cottage too: the way, in recent years, it had became so intensely just the two of them. The way that there were no excuses here for her and Greg's later failure to interest one another. *Tell me what you want*, he'd said to her on one trip, accusingly. He'd meant physically, of course. He was happy to try new things, he'd said. *You know what I like, you always have. Tell me what you like.* As though her physical pleasure was a secret she was using against him. But how to tell him that the things she found pleasing now were entirely unpredictable to her? It was new things, in these last few years, that had provided small jolts of pleasure. Early-morning, mizzled fields, walking the dog and a fat, rude glug of cuckoo spit attached to a blade of grass. Across the fence to the farm next door, the soft, pudendal muzzle of a horse. A gift from a friend of a new pair of gloves, carefully tailored, her hands warm inside them, her fingertips ticking with her pulse. How did any of these things translate into something she could say she *wanted*?

She heads downstairs, the dog following. She switches on heaters, cooks up a hot breakfast from what she has brought: flat mushrooms and tomatoes, grainy bread onto which she spreads great clots of pale butter. She washes her face, then dresses in the dull, comfortable things she has packed. She did once aspire to dressing well and had tried to choose colours that suited her. But whenever she saw photos she was always horrified. Her carefully selected clothes looked garish and ill-fitting and try-hard. She'd gotten rid of them years ago. She wears overalls for work, and even though Ewen is now in his twenties, at home she dresses in dark colours and denim—clothes that would forgive the smear of a child's hands and face, a uniform that had served her well in the final weeks of caring for Greg.

How she had loved those early years of mothering Ewen: the visceral pleasures of caring for his small body. The plump, pink skin of his cheeks. His drum of a belly. The constant wild babbling, the careering around. The abandon to intimacy with him and only him. The mess and the warmth and the smell of him.

And also: those early years had been totally unbearable. When Ewen was first born, she had watched in fear as he drifted towards sleep. His eyes would turn wide and still, his pupils seeming to pool, his eyelids fluttering then his eyeballs rolling back beneath them. It was difficult to tell whether he might be having a silent fit or an aneurysm. She was unnerved every time he went under. And when he got ill, which was often in those early years, it was even worse. When he was feverish, his face purpled. His fingertips would throb with heat as he pressed them, distractedly, morbidly, one by one, into her breasts. Why did you birth me, his fingers seemed to enquire, to suffer like this?

Wasn't it weird to think in this way? For every single thought to be followed by a contradictory one. To have no way to gauge whether you were happy or suffering. Schizoid—what was the old meaning of that word again? Its root was something to do with contradiction, wasn't it? But no, even that idea was wrong. It wasn't a schism in her thoughts and feelings, it was something different. Both things at the same time. Everything always at once. Is there a word for that?

Enough of this. The dog needs walking. And she needs to get to the beach. It's the start of spring, though you wouldn't know it. When she reaches the shore, the edges of the sea are freezing on the sand, a froth of fine ice briefly left behind by the tide. Wind-tears score her face and her eyelashes brittle. While the dog chases the waves, she pulls up her hood and turns back towards the line of the land. There are the dunes. And the small, hollow lookout tower at the side of her cottage. The trees, growing slanted, their branches forced into weird, horizontal gestures of longing by the wind. And behind them all, the heavy Cheviots, huge as the sky.

Over the past few summers, the campsite close by had occasionally cast brave folk up onto the beach, despite the bombastic yellow hazard signs at the edge of the dunes, which read: *WARNING: Localised quicksand. Do not touch metal objects. They may explode and kill you.* She and Greg had nodded to folk out walking on the dunes. They tended to be couples, or young families on a shoestring, or lone young men. They'd let children pet the dog and would tell them about the lookout tower—how it was left behind when they had practised the D-Day landings up here, how the beach had been churned up by mines so that even now there were pockets of quicksand and unpredictable patterns to the tides. They'd tell newcomers the best way to drive to Edinburgh and the paths to walk to Holy Island to avoid getting cut off by the sea. They'd leave the young couples be.

The dunes are empty of people today. No one else comes here at this time of the year. Her attention is drawn back to the beach by the dog barking at something on the sand up ahead. It looks as though a brown, viscous liquid has been spilled in two pools near the shore. Dirty waste of some kind? Oil, perhaps? As she gets closer, the spills resolve into jellyfish. Two enormous jellyfish, one even bigger than the other. A couple. She laughs.

Enjoying the idiocy of it, she hails them out loud: Daddy Jellyfish! Mummy Jellyfish!

But Daddy Jellyfish is badly hurt. She takes a step closer. He is split down the middle, his insides oozing through his filmy outer. His jelly is lustrous, the browny-gold of polished tiger's eye. I'll gather him up, she thinks, and she rushes at him with her hands. He doesn't sting her, but he is totally unmanageable. He slips around on her arms, and then folds over himself, dribbling like an undercooked omelette. Then his innards splatter onto the sand at her feet.

Shit! she shouts at the dog. What a mess.

She flings the half-empty disc of film away from her, and it deflates at the edge of the surf. The next wave will sweep him away.

I'm sorry, she says to Mummy Jellyfish.

She looks at her again: alone now, perfectly composed, her innards supple and lucent beneath her surface. She scoops her up too, more carefully this time. It's not easy, but she manoeuvres the jellyfish onto the sleeves of her jacket, getting the measure of her slipperiness. She walks to the edge of the sea and settles her in. She watches until the creature sinks, alone, into the deep grey.

Back at the cottage, she kicks the sand off her boots against the doorframe and fights the wind to open the door. The dog runs in ahead of her and shakes saltwater from his coat all over the sitting-room rug. Her hands have gone numb. She stands in the hall and watches them fingering the buttons of her coat. She climbs up to the bedroom and searches in her bag for Greg's jumper, the one he always brought to the cottage. She puts it on. The dog wanders in tight circles round the lounge, head low. Is he scenting for Greg?

The light flickers in the living room. Low on power. She goes through to the kitchen and turns pound coins into the meter so that she can start on the washing-up. The wind shrieks through the gaps in the windows. She looks out at the watchtower and the ice-blue sky around Holy Island. She listens to the garbled shanties whipping off the sea as she washes white waxy fat off the frying pan. Off the plate. Off the knife. Off the fork. She stops. She watches the foam bubbles slide back from the draining board down the sides of the sink and she lets the cold hold her here for a moment, lets it reach, big and unstoppable, around her. Soon enough it will be night. There are no soft domes of light, promising the mitigation of a town close by, on this horizon. The cottage is the deepest place of dark, making the shape of your hand in front of your own eyes a guess. The earth will turn black. The early lambs, sticky with blood, will be black. The sleeping gulls with heads under wings: black. The dunes and the sea and the massive Cheviots, all indistinguishable black.

How she hates being newly alone like this. This echo of cutlery in the sink. This nothingness wrought of years and years of hard work at togetherness. The impulse to make the contradictory chaos of her thoughts coherent, translatable to another, now totally obsolete.

And how she loves being newly alone. No one, now, to intrude upon her with demands of intimacy or legibility or care. Tonight, she will take whisky to bed and press the thin gold ring on her finger against her own soft flesh; and everything will pull together—her body, the sea, the black-gold sand, the lost jellyfish, the peat in her mouth, the call of the gulls, the whimper of the dog—and apart again, chaos and coherence, chaos and coherence, over and over, in the grief of the night.

Clean work

Late-blooming roses and petrol: that smell of the end of summer. I've just eaten lunch in the backyard. I should be back at my desk already—I'm behind again and I'll have to work tonight, once Lola's asleep. But I stay a moment longer. Dallying. That's a real word, a word someone must once have used, though I don't think I've ever met anyone who could be said to *dally*. The sunflowers that I planted with Lola out here are beginning to brown at the edges. I trail my fingertips across them. Big, radial flower-heads the same temperature as the air. The fur at the centre is sticky and glistening with sap. They feel warm-blooded. There are two wasps moving low to the ground. When one of them lands, exhausted, on a paving stone, the other homes in on it, putting its upper jaws straight to work.

I go back inside to make a coffee. Just as the kettle's starting to boil, I hear it again. That noise. A scrabbling sound, a scratchy, garbled movement somewhere in the internal workings of the kitchen.

♦

When I first got the keys to this house, I discovered that the previous owners had left me a bottle of champagne—the real stuff—and small traps set in all of the kitchen cupboards. The house was in a strange condition: a small Victorian redbrick terrace, with a smart new bathroom on the first floor, but the rest of the house left damp and mouldering. The previous owners had bought it as a doer-upper, the agent told me: *But now, sadly, are... no longer together. Doesn't it have wonderful potential?* The wallpaper was starting to peel away in the hallway, and the walls themselves were cold and chalky to the touch. The kitchen was the worst. When I stepped down into it, this low, narrow return at the back of the house, the smell hit straight away: green and fungal. I was pregnant with Lola then, and the smell made me gag. There were holes in the brickwork that had been filled with expanding foam. The floor tiles were laid straight onto the earth. No central heating in here and at every surface edge—the skirting boards, the join with the oven—there was a thin line of black sludge. When I moved in, I found that the cupboards produced a fine powdered mould that coated our plates and bowls. And there were slugs—great, ponderous slugs with frilled orange bodies, which left trails over the clean washing, across the baby grows that I had bought in a job-lot second hand, which I had boil-washed and smoothed out on the clothes horse, all clean and ready for Lola.

I had stayed cheerful, at first. The house's quirks were to my advantage. It needed some work, but that's why I could afford it. I was going to save up and scrub up and make the house right. We were going to live brightly, Lola and I, in a modernised terrace with clean surfaces and tightly sealed apertures. Look, hadn't I arranged everything? Hadn't I gotten a mortgage, by myself, against all the odds? Hadn't I saved and scraped and grafted on overtime? For when the baby arrived. For me and my Lola.

♦

I ring my mum to tell her about the scrabbling sound in the kitchen. I can tell that she's busy.

Mmm hmmm, she says. Old houses do make strange noises, you know, love.

I tell her that I've a feeling it might be a rat.

How do you know that? she says. Maybe it's a pigeon got into the roof space again and then back out? Can you smell anything?

I walk into the kitchen and put her on speaker-phone. I sniff deeply and then I listen for a long time, but there is no sound, and nothing I can smell above the ambient mould.

The next day, Lola's at nursery and I'm at my laptop working in the dining room when I hear it again. Scrabbling. A definite scrabbling inside the kitchen. I move into the doorway. Stand stock-still. The sound is coming from the carcass of a cupboard. I step closer. The sound is inside the cupboard next to the washing machine. Scratch scratch scratch. I'm too afraid to open the door, so I give the cupboard a hard kick and then I hear the creature scramble, claws slipping. Out of the kitchen window, I catch a glimpse of it as it runs across the yard, its thick brown tail disappearing under the back gate.

I call the first pest-control company that comes up online. I am told about the three-stage process for the elimination of rats:

1. The laying of poison.
2. The removal of dead rodents.
3. A full report on how to secure the property against future *infestation*.

I've only seen one rat, I say. I wouldn't call it an *infestation*.

Well, says the woman, rats rarely eat alone. If you've seen one, there'll be more.

How much is it then? I ask.

For the full three-step programme? That will be £400 in total including VAT. No hidden costs.

That's... more than I was expecting, I say. I'll have to think about it.

Her: Don't think about it for too long. Rats need to gnaw. They gnaw through electrics and cause twenty-five per cent of house fires. They carry hepatitis. They multiply quickly. You don't want to be thinking about it for long.

My mum comes round with a large rat trap and wire wool that she's bought at Barnitt's. We listen to the animal moving in the wall cavity in the kitchen and I stamp on the ground until it bolts again.

This isn't going to work, I say. What will we even do if we trap it? Where would we release it? They carry hepatitis, Mum.

I go to make Lola her tea. The rusks are in the kitchen cupboard at ground level and the porridge oats too. Mum plays with Lola, bouncing her on her lap. She's telling her the story of the Pied Piper, for fuck's sake.

Let's go out for tea, I say.

We eat chips sitting on a bench in town and then Mum says, Why don't you ring around in the morning? There must be a cheaper way of doing it. You might ask your dad for some help, you know?

I won't ask my dad for some help.

All night long, I'm googling rats on my phone. Infrared videos of them crawling round people's houses in the dark, climbing up chairs and table legs and into toilet-bowls to drink.

I wake up longing for the rat's total obliteration. Nothing left behind—the house destroyed. Scorched earth.

I dress Lola and take her to nursery. I pray that she doesn't repeat the word 'rat', which she said over and over before we went out, delightedly, pointing to the kitchen.

When I get back home, I put on my winter gloves and I clear the cupboards of food. Then I look through an old copy of *Local Link*. There are adverts for roof repairs and cleaners and clairvoyants and there, yes, there it is: Pest control.

While I wait for the rat man to arrive, I code documents into Xml. It's my job to make the text clean. I proofread and place tags around parts of articles, around lozenges within sentences, to make sure that they appear correctly when they're published online.

<title> <author> <date> <main text> / Scratch, scratch, scratch.

When I get thirsty, I go to the Londis on the corner and buy energy drinks rather than go back into the kitchen.

♦

Just after Lola was born, I bought a patch of Astroturf to lay out in the backyard. The yard is made of rough, uneven slabs, and each crack is filled with shards of broken slate and small stones. I wanted to give her one patch of something safe and green. I thought of her crawling on it, when she was big enough, or lying out in the sunlight. At the first touch of springtime warmth, flea eggs began to hatch in the Astroturf. It took me a long time to work this out—I thought the fleas were hatching in the carpet inside. I became suspicious of everyone who visited. I even made my mum strip off at the door, in case she was bringing them back from a client visit.

One evening, I looked into Lola's cot and discovered a flea fat with blood on her leg. I became demented then. I hovered over her at night with a bar of soap, which my mother said the fleas would stick to. I desired Lola's cleanness more than anything. I became a scrupulous angel of death. I shook flea powder everywhere. But flea powder is highly toxic. What would I do when Lola started to crawl? I hoovered the flea powder back up. I mopped and I mopped. Then I bought non-toxic traps instead: a tea light in the middle of a small metal circle covered with sticky paper that caught the fleas fast. Though they were still alive then, just stuck. So I crushed their bodies individually between my nails, bursting those little seeds of blood, scouring my hands after each one, until they were all gone.

♦

The rat man is small and polite. He pulls on rubber gloves when we enter the kitchen. I walk behind him. He thumps the kickboards until they give way and then he shines a small torch under each of the cupboards. The smell is bad when he does this: warm and close and animal. He finds fur and sweet wrappers that the rat has pulled inside, and, under another cupboard, faeces.

That's its toilet, he says. They're clean like that. They keep things separate.

We walk around the back of the house. He looks at the kitchen wall, at all the poorly filled gaps there.

Any of these, he says, could do it. A rat only needs fifteen millimetres to get inside. They can eat right through that expanding foam. I call it rat ice cream.

Then he looks around the backyard, finds a round hole in the earth next to the back gate.

That'll be it, he says. That's an active rat hole. You see how smooth it is? How the earth is clear all around it? Their fur is oily and when they're in and out, the oil makes the hole smooth and clean like that.

He lays poison. He puts some of it directly into the hole. Then he places trays full of the bright blue pellets under each of the kitchen cupboards. He rakes the poison with his gloved fingers as he settles the trays on the floor. Rats, he says, are neophobes. They don't like new things. We need to leave this ten days or so, to make sure that they've gotten used to it and then they'll take it.

And can I block the holes in the back wall now, I say, with wire wool? To stop them coming back in?

Best not to, he says. You don't know where they're nesting. Could be inside. Could be in your wall cavities. And if you block their escape route then once they've eaten the poison they'll die inside and the smell is very, very bad and there's no way to get rid of it.

♦

My uncle phones me. We haven't spoken since Christmas.

I hear you have a rat, he says. It doesn't matter if you kill it. There are always more.

There's excitement in his voice.

What you've got to do is work out where they're coming from and seal off the house.

Then my dad, who hasn't visited in months, arrives unannounced all the way from Beverley to walk the outside perimeter of the kitchen. He holds his hands behind his back.

I told you this house was substandard, he says. You're living in a Victorian slum. You're bound to have problems.

We have little to talk about these days, almost nothing we can find a consensus on. He sees any problem I have as the inevitable result of my poor decisions.

I'll come and do some cementing for you, he says, once they've taken the poison.

I tell the neighbours. Ruth from next door says to me, Don't feel bad. Don't feel bad about poisoning it. I'm vegan, and I'd kill a rat if it came in my kitchen.

The old-timer from across the road calls out to me one morning: How are your little friends?

I wait for the smell of death. My sister rings to tell me about the rats her boyfriend had in his old flat. About how he laid the poison and then went away for the weekend. When he came back, the flat seemed darker. He turned on the lights and discovered the windows black with flies. The smell, she says, was impossible to get rid of.

Then she tells me about another friend who used glue traps. For a few days there was nothing stuck to them. But one morning, there was a single bloodied claw stuck to the bottom of a trap. The rat had gnawed its way to freedom.

I tell her to stop talking to me about rats.

I buy scented candles and incense and spread them all over the house. The air inside tastes like soap.

♦

Before I bought this house, I lived in a top-floor flat in a converted fruit warehouse on the other side of the city with Stacey, my ex. A few months after we moved in, we were burgled by someone who had a key. They burgled us with a kind of frenzy, rifling through every drawer and cupboard, but also ripping open everything they could find: shirts were thrown onto the floor with the buttons ripped off, sealed packets of spaghetti and washing-up tablets had been torn open and spilled out, as though we might have had our valuables laminated inside them. The woman in the flat next door looked gratified when I said we'd had a break-in. She told us that at least ten people had been sleeping in the flat before we moved in. *Chinese*, she whispered in a significant tone. *You'd best call the landlord and get a locksmith in*, she said.

You get some jobs you have a bad feeling about, the locksmith had said while he was on his knees in the shared hallway, disarticulating the bottom lock. *Like, how do I know you're not the burglars? I mean, obviously you're not.*

He looked me and Stacey over, and we both felt inadequate.

But with other... clients, you arrive, and they've no proof the place is theirs. Divorces, other shady stuff. You wonder if you're being paid to lock someone out of their own home sometimes. So I'm thinking of retraining. To do something... decent. Something clean. You know.

Yes, I thought, when he said that. Yes, I know what you mean. My great-grandfather was a night soil man, collecting shit from outside water-closets as the dawn broke over Bradford each morning. My father is a public health inspector, dealing in abattoirs, drains, infestations, pestilent kitchens. My mother works in probation, dealing with the mess that comes after—and before—a crime. All I've ever wanted was clean work.

He carried on with the lock and I brought him coffee and then he said to me: *What do you do for work then?*

I was working a few different jobs back then, part-time, so I picked one. *I work in a library*, I said. *I shelve books at the university library in town.*

Have they got valuable books? he asked.

Some, I said, *in Special Collections.*

How do you protect them then?

We have reading rooms, I said. *And you have to apply for access. Some of the rarer things you can only see if you're supervised by an archivist.*

Nah, he said, *I mean from vermin. I'm thinking of getting into pest control, see. Been doing my research. Rodents, they're a problem in libraries. And moths too. It's a tricky business though.*

You've got to be careful. Even then you can get into trouble. You can't even look at a badger funny. If you catch a bird in a net, you're looking at thirteen months in jail.

♦

When the rat man comes back, he asks me if I have any holidays planned. I haven't.

I'm off to Portugal next week, he says. He's cheerful as he checks the poison under the cupboards.

Doesn't it bother you, I say, going under there?

These don't bother me, he says. It's the small ones that bother me. Cockroaches and bedbugs. Wasps. Coming into wasp season now. It'll be fumigations all afternoon.

The rat has taken the poison. The rat has eaten all of the blue pellets in one of the trays so now it will be dead or dying, he says. Fifteen pellets is all it takes. And as there's no smell, he's confident it's gone back outside. He'll come back in a few days' time, he says. I've to ring him if I hear or smell anything different.

♦

Autumn's here. Webs collecting in all the corners of the house, great fragile harvestmen descending from the light fittings. I've stopped trying to get rid of them and the spiders.

When the rat man comes for the final time, he removes the trays of poison and tells me to seal up the holes in the yard and the walls with wire wool and cement.

I listen for noises while I'm working at my laptop, and sometimes I hear a ticking sound near the sink. When I go into the kitchen, I stamp my feet and bang about. I've filled up the gaps as best I can. Every hole is stuffed with wire wool, particles of which adhered to my cheeks and lips afterwards and made them bleed.

I buy peppermint plants and strong-smelling oils to keep in the kitchen: a warding-off. I search and search for tiny traces of blue poison, trailing my fingertips along the floor-boards for any tiny toxic thing that Lola might find and eat.

Sometimes, at night-time, I still look for rats. As Lola whimpers, I search on my phone and click through to an article about the superior cognitive abilities and caring capacities of rats, about how, in experiments, they choose to feed their young rather than take cocaine, even if they've been made into addicts by the experimenters. I click through to a video of a *rat king*. A rat king is a ball of rats caught up, tails conjoined with filth. A rat king is a whole nest trapped together, terminally—the young to the old, the living to the dead.

♦

Every day, I clean up the articles that are sent to me, and Lola grows bigger. The mould in the kitchen is spreading again, and a sulphurous yellow fungus has begun to grow where the paint is peeling off the window frames. The wood there is sodden and comes away when I press it with my thumb-nail. I can't afford to do anything about it until next summer. The floorboards are damp now too, swelling and spongy underfoot. I catch Lola working away at one of them, peeling away a fat splinter with her keen fingernails and pushing it into her mouth before I can stop her.

At nursery pick-up time, I watch other people with their toddlers. Their faces bright in the cold, their bodies swaddled in new woollen clothes.

I love winter! one woman says to me. And being all cosy at home with them! Don't you?

The late afternoon is cold-blue hush. It's the desolate hour just before winter nightfall. I walk slowly with the pushchair. The evening rolls out ahead of me: tea-time and bath-time, scooping spaghetti hoops from the floor, wiping Lola's face, taking off her soiled clothes, folding her fat, damp nappy into the bin. The tender, tedious rituals of making her clean again, the lick of thick cream on her bottom, the fresh nappy, the almond lotion on her belly and legs. I'll nurse her to sleep—that pain when she first latches still like a lance, but it softens as she drifts, until I can barely feel she's there. I'll press my nose to the skin of her scalp then. Baby soap and something else, something sweet and fungal that I breathe in deep.

♦

It's the new year when I hear it again. The scrambling sound, the scratchy, garbled movement deep in the internal workings of the kitchen. I move into the doorway. The sound is coming from the carcass of a cupboard. I step closer. The sound is definitely inside of the cupboard next to the washing machine. The same place as before. This time, I want to see it. I reach out. Hand on cupboard door. Slowly, slowly open it. Frozen. Both of us frozen for one long moment. Then—tiny tics of attention. Sleek brown fur rippling with movement. Sharp eyes. A well-fed, supple body. The creature collides with the cheese grater and then drops away down the back of the cupboard.

I'm breathless afterwards. I think about calling the rat man. But I don't. Not yet. She looked so clean and fat and vivid, our rat.

Fifteen pellets is all it takes.

Lying in bed that night, I try not to listen. I try to pretend there's nothing to hear. Just the little murmurs that Lola makes in her sleep. The echo of a pigeon in the chimney breast. The house ticking as it contracts inside the cold night. Don't listen to the scuttle in the wall. The scrabble of claws somewhere inside the house.

I lie awake until the sound moves away and then I fall into a dream. Inside of the dream, Lola is nursing all night long, her mouth smooshed to my breast. Inside of the dream, my milk runs blue in my veins, my milk runs in poisoned rivulets towards her: sweet and luminous.

Transcendent inadequacies

When the girl has finished playing the piece—fudging the fingering, going faster the less certain she becomes of the notes, ending suddenly with a chord that seems to surprise even her—he leans back in his chair, lifting a pencil to his mouth. The pencil bears his name, embossed in gold: *Kenneth Scholes, Music Teacher*. He traces the little rubber at the end of its shaft against the edge of his bottom lip.

After a long pause, he speaks.

You're the kind of person, he says to the hunched girl at the piano, who would go into a shop and ask for one doughnut and one doughnut and one doughnut, rather than for three doughnuts. You're the kind of person who makes things more difficult for herself.

The girl clasps her hands in her lap and stares at the keys.

I'm not allowed to eat doughnuts, she says. Trans fats make you stupid.

On another occasion he holds his head in his hands as she attempts a simple piece of Bach. It's the fingering again, all over the place, producing unexpected and unfortunate emphases. The more mistakes she makes, the quicker she hurtles through the piece. He sits still for a long time after the noise is over.

What I'm beginning to think, Coral, he says, is that you have a comic gift. You're an absurdist.

Thank you, she says, uncertainly.

Another time, Coral's mother brings her younger sister to the house while Coral has her piano lesson. Coral's mother cleans Mr Scholes's kitchen, lounge and home office to pay for Coral's lessons. There is the usual silent pause after Coral has played her piece as Mr Scholes leans back in his chair, contemplating the performance. Coral's sister, Molly, an indefatigable two-year-old, repeatedly whacks the toy xylophone in the next room.

Mr Scholes leans forward, lowering his voice conspiratorially. I can already tell, Coral, he says, that your sister has considerably more natural musicality than you.

♦

Coral sits at the kitchen table doing her maths while her mother makes cheesy spuds.

She's been trying for weeks to talk to Mum. She keeps bottling it. She'll have to use the countdown technique Mum taught her to deal with The Dreads. Five, four, three, two, one—

I think I want to stop piano lessons, Coral says.

Her mother doesn't turn around. Her hands don't stop working. The oil from the potato skins makes her busy fingers gleam. Then she says: Did you have a difficult lesson, love?

It's just... I'm not very good at it, Mum.

No one's good at anything in the early stages, Coral. Learning things is hard. It takes years to be good at something. But we're not quitters, are we? We keep going, don't we?

How many times has her mother said this in the last year? So many times. It's been her mantra since Dad put his clothes in bin bags and moved in with Aunty Tracey. *We keep going, don't we?* Her mum works three jobs now, plus occasional cleaning to accumulate local favours, like cheaper childminding and extra maths tutoring and the piano lessons from Mr Scholes.

What does Mr Scholes say, Coral? I bet he doesn't say you're no good?

Coral's mum stabs each potato efficiently with a fork.

He says...

What does Mr Scholes say? It's mostly silence. And then his considered, cutting pronouncements.

She'll just tell it straight: He says Molly has considerably more natural musicality than me.

Well, Coral's mum says, he's joking, Coral! He can be very dry, Mr Scholes can. Mr Trevors says the piano will help with your maths, and the maths will help with your scholarship exams.

Coral's mum still hasn't turned around. She's cleaning the kitchen surfaces now and then she'll put the spuds in the oven then there'll be washing to put on and when tea is over and she's sent Coral up to read to Molly, Coral knows her mother will open her laptop on the kitchen table to start working again. If she wakes in the night, Coral sometimes creeps down the stairs to check on her. She's usually sitting at the laptop, the light from the screen making her face bright but colourless. Corpse-like. Does she sleep at all now?

If you're feeling worried about it, why don't you try doing some extra practice, Coral's mum says. Ask Mrs Richards if you can stay back an extra evening at school to use the piano more?

She finally turns around.

What do we do, Coral, if we feel like we're being beaten by something?

We work harder, Coral says.

Yes, you work harder. So you don't end up like me. So you don't have to do all the crappy jobs that I do.

But you work so hard, Mum, Coral says. And you still have to do the crappy jobs.

Coral regrets saying this instantly. Her mum hunches at the countertop. Totally still for a moment. Panic rushes through Coral. Her mum doesn't cry or swear though. She just sighs and then clatters about with a baking tray.

Yes, she says, but I never had your brain or your chances, did I, Coral?

Coral continues with her weekly lessons. The pattern remains the same: each week she plays her piece and there is a long silence as Mr Scholes leans back in his chair and contemplates his response. Coral learns to predict when he is about to deliver his verdict: satisfaction puckers his mouth in the moment before speech. *The problem with you, Coral*, his assessment often begins; or, *The thing I've come to realise about you, Coral...* Coral's problems are myriad: she lacks consistency; she is incapable of a measured approach; she is easily panicked and often reckless. For a long time,

Coral keeps alive the hope that one day one of Mr Scholes's pronouncements will be followed by an invigorating encouragement. This is how things work at her new school, where Coral now has her scholarship place. The girls there—who go to department stores rather than the market to buy their clothes, and who wear lip-gloss that they've researched online rather than fished out of the £1 basket at the side of the soap-and-household-detergents stall—accept chastisements in class in a beatific manner and then bitch about it together later. Mademoiselle Saunders raps on your desk and decries your pronunciation, making you say a phrase over and over, but then she'll congratulate you, enthusing in French when you get it right. Coral should be very grateful and proud, Mum says, to be allowed to go to the school. Coral has not yet mastered the expression that captures these two seemingly contradictory attitudes. At any rate, with Mr Scholes, she waits and waits, but there never is a *bon mot*. And by her fifth year of learning to play the piano, Coral begins to feel a strange excitement when she plays something particularly badly in her lesson. What will Mr Scholes say today? What personal flaw will he be able to detect through her bodged fingering? What transcendent inadequacy will he decipher in her failed syncopation?

One afternoon—a sticky-hot day in the summer holidays—Coral walks alone to her piano lesson. Mr Scholes lives on the other side of town, a good half an hour away from her house, past the Quaker School for Girls where she has her scholarship (grateful and proud, grateful and proud), on a leafy street behind the cathedral. In her own area, the roads are narrow and more uniform. There are no front gardens or communal squares or lawned crescents; the houses stand together, hunched convivially. Over here, the houses are matching semis with long driveways, or they are grand white terraces with wrought-iron balconies. They make her think of celebrity parties that end in disaster—bodies floating in swimming pools or impaled on sharp railings after balcony falls or slumped in designer bathrooms ODing—though she knows that celebrities don't party in northern market towns, much to the regret of the girls at school. Still, there is a deathly glamour to the houses on this side of town.

It's good to be out in the sun walking alone and to not have to worry about Molly for a bit. Coral looks after Molly most mornings in the summer. It's not that they don't have fun. Coral makes them toast fingers with peanut butter, and sometimes they eat them in bed and watch cartoons together on Coral's phone. Molly still smells like she did when she was a baby sometimes—sweet and soft and milky. But Molly is a biter. So when Coral takes her out, she has to be extra careful. Sometimes there is a warning—Molly's head will rear back and there's a moment when Coral can intervene. This happened at the park last week with a little boy who'd pushed in front of her for the slide. Molly reared back and was about to go for the boy's shoulder and Coral whipped her up and away just in time. But often Molly's just too quick. If it's too late and she's fastened on, Mum has taught Coral how to pinch Molly's nose to get her to release. Mum says Molly's acting out instead of putting her energy into developing properly. She's been slower to talk and write than Coral was. Mum wants Coral to do educational activities with Molly in the summer holidays. But sometimes, Coral thinks Molly might already be smarter than the both of them. They were in the supermarket a little while back and Mum dropped a glass jar of beetroot onto the hard floor. There was a lot of noise and fuss and Mum apologising and flapping, and they both took their eyes off Molly. Then someone was screaming. Molly was halfway down the aisle with her teeth sunk into the thigh of a man, right through his polyester trousers. *I didn't touch her*, he shouted, *I didn't do anything*. And then he bolted.

Here it is: Mr Scholes's smart front garden, and the path to his house.

Coral checks her clothes on the doorstep, to make sure she's neat and there's no VPL, and then she rings the bell.

You're early, Coral, he says to her when he appears at the door, and he makes even this sound like a fundamental failure of her character. You can come in, but you'll have to sit quietly in the kitchen while Lottie finishes her lesson.

Coral sits at the table and flits though the chats on her phone, trying not to listen in on the piano room. But after a little while, she has to lay her phone down on the table. What is this girl Lottie playing? The music is dreamy and complex. Sometimes Mr Scholes plays pieces on his stereo, examples of good technique or interesting interpretation. Perhaps he's playing a recording now? But the music is too vivid and near to her to be a recording. It's so strange and discordant, this music coming from the other room. It makes something swell in Coral's throat. By the time the piece has finished, she's holding her breath. She listens for what might be happening on the other side of the wall. Silence, for an unbearably long time. He's doing it. She can picture him doing it in there. He's leaning back now, searching for the right critique of that brilliant playing.

And then she hears it happen: the low, muffled sound of Mr Scholes's admonishing voice.

The doorbell rings and a woman lets herself into the house. Just walks right in without a please or a thank you. She sits down at the kitchen table and directs a tight-lipped smile towards Coral. The woman is wearing white trousers and she smells amazing. Can this be Lottie's mother? She doesn't look like anyone's mother.

When the girl comes out of the piano room, Coral stands up, clutching her carrier bag full of music to her chest.

Mr Scholes calls through: You can come in now, Coral.

The other girl has her books in a music case and stands at the side of the kitchen table for a moment. She's older than Coral, though she wears no make-up and her clothes are weirdly childlike. She's wearing a loose pinafore dress. Her throat and her cheeks are flushed.

Well? says the woman.

There's a lot of work to do on my action, the girl says quietly. Mr Scholes says that I can't attack properly.

The sound from the woman is barely audible: a little cluck of disapproval in the back of her throat.

Coral stares at Lottie, not yet able to move. She knows she should do something. But she has no idea what. The girl shuffles past her and then follows the woman out of the house.

For weeks afterwards, Coral thinks of the girl. She thinks of her at night when she settles Molly after a nightmare and the foxes are coughing outside and Mum is clack-clacking at her keyboard downstairs with her dead face. She thinks of that music, of the rush of feeling when Lottie was playing that rose in her like panic. She replays the encounter with

Lottie, thinking of all the things she could have said or done. How she could have told the girl's mother that she'd never heard anyone play like Lottie. How she could have hugged the girl, or held her hand—though that would have been weird. How she could have whispered to her, *You're good, really good at this. Your playing made me want to cry or run away*. But she didn't say or do any of those things, did she?

♦

When Molly turns six, they have a party with chocolate teacakes and the posh crisps, and Mum suggests that it's time for Molly to take up an instrument. Mum has invited Mr Trevors, Coral's old maths tutor, to the party. She used to clean for him too, but now she goes over without her cleaning things and he's giving Molly tuition for free all the same. Mr Trevors stands close to Coral's mother and occasionally rests his hand on the small of her back. Cold violence is what Coral feels when she looks at him, though he was always kind to her in the maths lessons and good at explaining things.

It's good for your brain, learning an instrument, Coral's mum says. Isn't it, Mr Trevors? There've been studies. It improves your maths.

Molly's toddling thuggishness has developed into an intense, destructive concentration. At bedtime, she hooks Coral's neck with her arms, bringing them forehead to forehead, and then she chants: Iloveyoulloveyoulloveyoullovcyou. Molly is ardent in all of her activities. She snaps pencils when she draws. She scores the table when she tries to write. She's brushed grooves into her milk teeth.

It's worked for you, hasn't it, Coral, love, the maths and the piano lessons? I think they really helped with the scholarship.

Coral and her mother are in Mr Scholes's kitchen as Molly's first piano lesson begins. Mum is cleaning the hob. Coral is sitting at the table listening intently as Molly hits the notes of the piano. She is hitting them so hard that the sound dies away almost immediately. The notes are minor catastrophes: the clang of a blunt instrument on metal, the clang of broken machinery. Coral can hear Mr Scholes's voice rising as Molly continues to strike the keys. She imagines him on the other side of the wall, unable to lean back in his chair, unable to retain his composure, unable to keep quiet as Molly lashes out at his piano.

Last night, Coral put Molly to bed as usual. She read her her favourite story—twice. And then she asked her, *Are you excited about your first piano lesson, Mols?*

Molly's eyes were dilating dreamily as they always did when she was close to sleep. Her hair was flat and wet from her bath. Her cheeks were pink and damp. She looked angelic, but she was still that little biter deep down.

Listen, Coral had said, shaking Molly from her drowsiness. *This is important, Mols.*

Molly's eyes widened. *What Corrie*? she said. *What?*

It's very important that you get your attack right in the piano lesson. When you hit the keys, you've got to do it as hard as possible. With all your strength, Molly. Hit me like you're going to hit those keys.

Coral held her palms upwards towards her sister.

Go on, hit the keys.

Molly balled one fist and brought it down.

Harder! Much harder, Mols! I know how strong you really are.

Molly wheeled her arm around behind her head and then brought it down on Coral's palm, properly hard.

Good, said Coral. *You need to use all your strength tomorrow. Whatever Mr Scholes says. You keep showing him you can attack the keys, okay? You keep hitting the piano as hard as you can whatever happens. Understand, Mols?*

Molly had nodded. When she finally fell asleep, her fists were still balled tight.

Mr Scholes is shouting in the piano room.

Christ, says Coral's mother, turning around from the oven. Do you hear that?

Mr Scholes is shouting as the same note continues to strike, over and over.

I think I'm going to have to go in there, Coral's mum says. Can you hear that?

Coral can hear it alright. Mr Scholes is really shouting now: Careful—careful—stop—stop it—Jesus, stop it! As the note continues to sound, again and again.

When Coral's mother opens the door to the piano room, Coral is right behind her. Mr Scholes is up on his feet. He's standing behind Molly. He has hold of Molly's right hand and is bending her arm backwards. The angle looks painful. But Molly's other hand is still free—and in a burst of movement, she wheels it round from behind her like a shot-putter, then smashes her fist down onto the keys. Many notes sound at once, and then the notes die away, leaving a whining noise in their wake. The noise left behind is coming from Mr Scholes and it continues to sound as he drops Molly's arm and stumbles backwards.

You get your hands off her, Coral's mother shouts. I will fucking have you!

Then there is a blur of movement and noise as Coral's mother darts forward and sprays Mr Scholes with the oven cleaner and Molly wheels both her arms freely again, striking at the piano. This one clear image Coral will always remember: Molly, grinning up at her with happy ferocity, as she continues to hammer the keys.

Days clean

Ryan notices things about me. He notices things about me and he likes to tell me the things that he notices. In the middle of cutting my hair, he'll pause, deliberate over his wording. *Your hair is an unusual colour*, he said to me the first time he cut it. *It's not mousey, not really. It's a dull colour but unusual. Mink. That's what I'd call it. Don't I remember you from school?* And he let a lifted clump of my hair fall back against my face with satisfaction. Another time, he asked me if I knew that I had a fine line of down along my jaw. *They call it peach-fuzz*, he said. He stroked the side of my cheek with closed scissors. *One of the girls could sort that out for you*, he said. *We do derma-blading now.* He noticed that my incisor teeth were sharply pointed, and that they could be capped, which would make me look softer. At my appointment last week, he told me he'd noticed me running near his house. *Kim has pissed off to Spain for a bit*, he said, pulling knots through my fringe and looking at his own reflection. *You should come over*, he said. *You should stop off for a drink when you're on one of your runs.* He was still looking at himself in the mirror.

I'm meant to do things like this. I am supposed to find ways to take care of myself—like getting a haircut. These things are on my list. When I feel restless or anxious, when I'm heading towards the danger zone, I'm supposed to try one of the following:

Take five deep breaths
Call a friend
Take a hot shower
Watch a film
Write in a journal
Go for a run
Squeeze ice cubes
Snap an elastic band against your wrist

Today I was on an early. My shift finished at lunchtime. I've done my breathing exercises and I've already taken a long shower. I called Chloe, but she'll be sleeping because she was on a late. What I usually do when the evening stretches dangerously ahead of me like this is: I watch Netflix and manipulate my appetite. I know exactly what to eat to stave off hunger for a short while, so that I'll feel it again soon and have something to concentrate on. Half a Bounty bar can see me through forty minutes. Then the hunger gnaws back, and I prepare the other half, eating it slowly. *Taking care of myself.* Sometimes I go to the Oasis every hour. I cruise for Bombay mix, celery and hummus, Kettle chips. Nothing too bulky, nothing that will keep me sated for long. Two hundred and eighty-nine days. I am two hundred and eighty-nine days clean.

Today I can't make myself feel hungry. I portioned out Ryvita and peanut butter, but I still can't summon an appetite. I keep remembering things about Ryan. Like: we used to gather after school in small, antagonistic groups on the railway embankment. Ryan was two years above me, and one summer evening his group of fit, dishevelled lads made a fire and then flickered their lighters against the polyester blazer of the boy who had been pushed up a year and was taking his exams early, and a spark caught against his hair and he stopped laughing along with them and ran all the way past us, careering down the embankment, slapping at his forehead.

I need to stop this. Memories put me right in the danger zone.

Ryan has done well for himself. Some of the old industrial buildings further along the valley, the canal-side warehouses and mill, have been converted into flats for people who commute to Manchester and Leeds, and Ryan's salon is popular with that crowd—there's a spa in the outbuildings and groups of women come for the afternoon to sit in hot tubs and have their nails painted. Ryan doesn't notice things about them. Or if he does, he conceals it. I've heard him talking to them while I wait in the salon, and he tells them flattering lies about their hair texture and their hydration levels.

Stop it. Stop dwelling on things.

It's freezing out, but I need to clear my head. I need to run. I change into my good kit quickly, and then I'm out the door. I try not to go too fast at first, though my body wants to accelerate. You can hurt yourself when it's this cold. I settle into a rhythm. One two, one two. I know exactly where Ryan's house is. At the very top of the valley there's a new development of five exclusive redbrick homes looking out over the village. I'm running towards it. It looks like it might snow, and there'll be a good view from up there. Also, there's a good long hill ahead, and I need a decent incline to work against. And what if I were to stop off at Ryan's house? Wouldn't that count as self-care? A conversation with a friend? I've always liked to see the inside of people's homes, to discover the ways they betray their mawkish or squalid or ruthless tendencies through glassware and ornaments, pets and filthy carpets, empty space and blank art.

Maybe these are reasons to go there. Maybe they're just pretexts.

By the time I get to the top of the valley the sky has clotted to purple and tiny flakes of snow are prickling my cheek-bones. *Your hair has a tendency to frizz*, Ryan once noticed. I must be frizzing right now. I stand outside his house for a while, wondering if he's out. The large windows are dark, but his car is in the drive. I'm about to carry on running when he opens the front door.

You coming in then, he says.

I'm glad when we go to bed. Ryan doesn't have the heating on and the rooms are anonymous as a show home's. I can feel my muscles tightening up instantly. He's kept the place immaculate in Kim's absence, and he gives me the tour, flicking the lights on in each room and then off again. The house showcases a blandness so thorough it must be masking something truly obscene. The walls are painted yellowish cream. The kitchen and dining room display large pictures of pasta and street cafes. The bathrooms are chronically tiled. We stand in the living room in the thin light of dusk, breath almost clouding, while I refuse a drink and he downs three shots of vodka.

He turns on one lamp when we get to the bedroom. Ryan's penis is thin and very long, and his thrusts are very precise, so that being fucked by him is like being repeatedly stung by a large insect. When he's finished, he uses his mouth and I curl my hands up until the sensation comes back and I can feel my blood blooming in my lips, little ticking pulses everywhere.

Two hundred and eighty-nine days. I am two hundred and eighty-nine days clean.

Afterwards, he lies back on the bed and starts noticing things again. You're skinny, he says, but fleshy too.

Neither assertion is a compliment.

You were really good at running, I remember that much, he says, as though I've asked him what he remembers, as though I want him to remember, when in fact I'm lying silently, trying very hard to think of nothing.

Didn't you nearly make it at some big event? Like, the Olympics? I mean, not the Olympics, but something? How do you get from that to... you know?

I'm a cautionary tale that's been passed around the village, I know that much already. There's a lot I could tell him. But what would be the point? Ryan gets absolutely shitfaced every weekend—he once asked me if I'd ever tried a spirit called Unicum, told me that he'd drunk so much of it he'd almost gone blind, that it tasted like de-icer and that he wasn't sure the lad serving them hadn't just given them all antifreeze as a joke—but he's waiting, now, to be sanctimonious.

I've learned that if you tell a person about one bad thing, then they might be sympathetic. If you tell them you were injured, for instance, and that's why he first gave you the Oramorph, they might give you kindly meant and totally redundant advice about pain management and opioids. When you tell them the next bad thing that happened, they start to glaze over. And by the time you tell them the third bad thing, they've turned against you. One bad thing can happen to anyone. But several bad things in a row? That's a character flaw.

You can stay here if you want, Ryan says, but you'll have to sleep in the spare room. This is my and Kim's room.

When I walk back down the gravel road towards the village, the sky is properly dark and the snow has dissolved to almost nothing. The factory in the valley-bottom is juddering through the start of the night shift. When we were at school, he tripped me up once, Ryan did. I've only just remembered that. *Watch where you're going,* he said, and then he gave me a hard shove and caught me again, pulling me up, laughing all the while. *That means he likes you*, another girl said to me after he'd walked away. *That's what they do when they like you.*

I start to warm up again and I go through the list of affirming thoughts that my support worker told me to memorise. I was, for a while, the fastest female under-16 in the Yorkshire region. I passed all of my GCSEs. Dogs usually trust me straight away. My cousin's little girl, when she was small and couldn't breathe for croup, once let me hold and calm her—she checked her breath against mine in the moonlight of a pub car park and I felt the pulse in her cheek beat and then settle against my throat. My mum says she has forgiven me. My mum says she has forgiven me. I am two hundred and eighty-nine days clean.

I count the beats of my feet on the cold tarmac. One two, one two. The days are shorter now, but that doesn't stop them feeling long. How will I fill the hours tonight if sleep won't come? What if I can't stop the memories and mistakes from returning? I run a little faster. The hill is behind me and my feet rush downwards. I used to train by doing hill runs—that rollercoaster of gravity, the vertigo of speed. He used to tell me to eat spaghetti beforehand—makes it easier to throw up when you're training properly hard. Stop remembering. Fucking stop remembering. One two, one two. Two hundred and eighty-nine days.

I'm down in the valley-bottom—I can hear the river through the woods—I'm really getting into my stride, when I see the glint of something on the road up ahead. Cat's eyes? I slow down to have a proper look. *Actual* cat's eyes. There's a cat crouched a few metres ahead of me. I pull up. It's not a tame cat. Not from the look it's giving me. There are feral kittens born in these woods each spring, their fur thick with bluebell dust and fleas. The cat stares at me in terror, and then she darts round to her tail, grooming it viciously. I stay very still, though my breathing is loud. Why is she not moving off the road? She's still going at her tail, grooming and biting it. Then I see—her tail is flattened to the tarmac. She's been caught by a car. She's stuck by her own matted tail to the road. She savages her hind quarters again. There is blood on one of her white cheeks. I take a step towards the cat and she freezes, hunching even lower. Then she turns on her tail with a horrible ferocity and with another bite she is free, spinning in a circle and veering off into the woods, her front legs at a gallop, her back legs stumbling. Left behind on the road is most of her tail—a mat of fur and blood—and there, in the centre, the glimmer of a tiny connective bone, like a pearl.

I run. I run past what's left behind. I've seen cats without tails who have looked rakish and happy enough, so why shouldn't she be? I run up the zig-zag road all the way to the other side of the valley, two hundred and eighty-nine, one two, one two, until I find snow again, tiny, stinging flakes, at the very top of Lamb Lane. From here, I can see right to the other side of the moor. The five redbrick houses are in outline on the top. There is only one light on in Ryan's house.

I will not go up there again.

Air surges into my lungs, cold and vivid. *Life's not kind*, my nan used to say to me, when I was at my worst and she nursed me with equal parts love and anger, my nan who was born in this valley-bottom, who is buried down there next to the church and the river: *Whoever made you to think that life was kind was lying.*

I know, Nan, I know that life is not kind. But there's no use for a merciful God, not while you've teeth in your own jaws.

I am two hundred and eighty-nine days clean.

The chrysalides

At first, we walked the pavements of the empty city in circuits. We were allowed out for one hour each day but the parks and gardens in the city centre were locked, so we stared through the railings at spring flowers, trying to sight hyacinth and crocuses, sanitising our hands immediately after each contact.

Nia looked behind us as we walked, eyeballing the new emptiness.

Mama, she said, why are we *alone*?

After a few weeks, we stopped going into town—the closed shops and bare market stalls and echoey arcades were no longer a novelty. Instead, we paced the streets around our flat, and sometimes we walked next to the river, along a path that used to be congested with daytime drinkers and empty nitrous-oxide cartridges and now incorporated harried parents taking lunch-hour walks with their children. We observed our neighbours with new interest. Some had sellotaped pictures of rainbows in their windows. One house displayed a *Daily Joke*, which I found depressing but Nia liked me to read to her, and which she treated like a puzzle: Hmmm, why *did* the onion need help, Mama?

In the evenings, I watched the people living around us as their lights came on. I watched the couple in the house diagonally opposite—one watching News 24 on the downstairs telly, and one watching something else in the bedroom upstairs. I watched the boy in the attic room smoking at dusk as bats flittered in the sky above him. And I watched the old man take to his bed. I felt uneasy watching him, and yet, each night, before I closed the curtains, there he was, unavoidable: directly opposite, propped up and illuminated, the ceramic cats on the shelves next to him watching too as he lay back on the pillows.

Later in the spring, my sister sent a gift for Nia through the post: a large box, containing a see-through plastic cup and other arcane apparatus. At the bottom of the cup was a layer of dense sand-coloured material that looked like fudge. This cup apparently contained caterpillars. At first, the creatures were hard to make out. Five small, brown animals, inert, almost indistinguishable from the fudge. The instructions told us that the caterpillars would eat this dense material once they had 'woken up'. Nia and Sam chose a place for the cup on the carpet in a shady corner of the flat.

The next morning, we checked on the caterpillars. They were still, still.

Why aren't they awake yet? Nia asked.

They're just starting to wake up, Sam said. It'll take some time. Let's check again tomorrow.

I don't know how we filled our day then. Nia had stopped wanting to go outside at all. The prohibitions on touch, the playgrounds cordoned off like crime scenes, the way I ferociously cleaned her hands after she touched anything: the disappointments of being outside had become too great. Perhaps Nia practised her writing. She had started to compose letters, but she was writing on a different plane, so the N from her name was written sideways, looking more like a Z. Perhaps she played with her dolls while I tried to work, making them sneeze again and again, and nursing them with fierce admonitions. I often felt tired and dematerialised during those weeks—that the dolls' needs and the supposedly urgent documents in my inbox and Nia's chatter and the timelines that I scrolled through populated the flat, and that I was hardly in it at all. There is a particular loneliness that comes of being only in the company of a child. I was losing the ability to communicate in adult terms. What have you been up to then? my mum would sometimes ask on the phone. The baby-doll, Gummy, has allergies and I've mostly been repeatedly taking her to the imaginary pharmacy and sometimes wrapping her head in toilet-paper bandages when she bleeds, I had to stop myself from replying.

The highlight of my weeks back then was a yoga class held via Zoom on Tuesday evenings. It was run by a woman who lived on the ring road not far from us. I found myself tuning in to the relay of sirens in our respective backgrounds. An ambulance would pass our flat, the siren blaring in real time and then fading away, only to enter her screen as background sound. Sometimes it went the other way: the siren would start in the background of her video, and then repeat on the road outside me. I listened carefully for it, this proof that me and the woman were in the same city at the same awful time.

I wondered if the old man could see me doing yoga. I worried that, as he couldn't move, he had no choice but to watch me attempting a sun salutation. Things were getting worse for him. I knew that because there was almost always someone there with him now, in the daytime at least. The healthcare workers visited in pairs: young women in dark blue overalls and bright blue gloves and medical masks. Another elderly man often sat with him and ordered himself Deliveroo at mealtimes. At night, it was just me and those porcelain cats watching on. It was an old-fashioned illness; I knew that much because he was still at home and he was allowed his one visitor. He was wearing a mask that connected him to oxygen. Sometimes, I thought I could see the whites of his eyes as he struggled for breath.

A few days after they had arrived, the caterpillars began to make themselves apparent. They began hunching their way across the fudge-food and up the transparent plastic walls of the cup. Shrugging all over the place with their whiskery little bodies. We watched them avidly.

Can they be my pets? Nia said.

Sam said: We'll have to set them free, you know, Ni. We'll have to let them out of a window, or take them down to the river. So they can't really be pets. People never really *own* animals.

Okay, said Nia, but can I touch them first?

Her desire to touch something other than us had reached pitiful levels: *Can we go to a farm so that I can stroke a chicken? Please, Mama? Can I have a puppy or a kitten?* The geese in the city were nesting in new places—on the empty train station platform, in the middle of a pavement in an empty shopping precinct—and one day we walked past a whole gaggle marauding across a road. Nia tried to touch one. She was disappointed when it ran away. *You said they were fierce*, she said to me accusingly. *How can I get one to peck me?*

I too was experiencing a libidinous, doomed longing for contact. I found myself fantasising about the time in my life when I used to just fall into other people; when a night out could end anywhere—with four of you strewn across the softer surfaces of someone's flat, with dawn spilling across an alien bed and the touch of a stranger gently waking you. Once, a friend and I had missed our last train home and had no money for a taxi, so I used my cash card to gain entry to the foyer of a Natwest and we slept there curled up on each other. At the time, it had felt like a low ebb. Now it seemed like the highpoint of my life.

I began to watch the contacts that the old man received—the daily care from the pairs of strangers who came to his door, the doctors who arrived to administer drugs directly into his veins, the other man who sat at his bedside and held his hand—with a deep fascination that was almost like longing.

The caterpillars grew with astonishing speed. In just a few days they had doubled in size. They shed their skins in the cup several times. They began to produce silk, which webbed from one side of the cup to the other. Their whitish excreta collected beneath them. Their bodies became fat and intelligent and they moved around each other impatiently.

One evening, when Nia had just gone down, Sam glanced at the cup and saw it happening. Come see this, he said to me. One caterpillar had hunched its way to the lid of the cup and was suspending itself. Then the others followed, with uncanny synchronicity. Over the course of just a few minutes, each one crawled to the lid and fixed itself there. They hung, all five of them, perfectly still.

While we were sleeping, they bound themselves into cocoons. They became chrysalides. Hardened and reptilian.

We noticed little flecks of gold beginning to form on their exteriors. Each chrysalis was dotted with it. It was bewildering. They were making gold from the sludge in a cup and the poor light in our living room.

As Nia and I were watching, counting the little metallic horns, one of the chrysalides began to jerk around.

Christ, I said. What's going on in there?

It kept on jerking. It made me think of a hanging.

I thought you said they liquefied in the cocoon? I said to Sam. How is that one still moving?

It is... surprising, Sam said. It mustn't be fully... melted down yet.

Sam gave me the significant wide-eyed look he does to secretly say: *Is Nia ok? Should we let this continue?*

She was watching the horrible scene, completely rapt.

I shrugged back at him, which is my silent sign for: *I have absolutely no fucking clue.*

It took several minutes, but then the jerking stopped.

There were days of stillness then. The creatures hung together in their tiny gold-studded sarcophagi.

When I next walked into town, I discovered large, laminated sheets in an empty square. The sheets were marked up with statistics on the numbers of Black people killed by police in the US and the UK. There were no large demonstrations in our town, but people had taped posters about police killings to lampposts too. When I got back home, I told Sam about it. I felt that this might be some kind of tipping point. The world was waking up to what was going on. Something had just made gold from the sludge in a cup and the poor light in our living room. Didn't that prove that things could change, even in the most constrained conditions? In fact, that radical change was inevitable, was actually part of nature?

No, Sam said. He was brittle in his response. I was making outlandish comparisons, he said. The change we had just witnessed wasn't mammalian. Mammals were different. Mammals couldn't make gold from shit. And why did I think that animal processes were metaphors? They weren't. They were specific and real, he said, and to think that human change is inevitable is complacent. People were working for change. They were working really hard. It didn't just *happen*.

The instructions told us that after ten days we should transfer the chrysalides into the butterfly house—a large net tube that sprung out of its packaging like a miniature throw-up tent. We were now to remove the lid of the cup and transfer it to a holder, so that the cocoons could continue to hang from it inside the house. This was a precarious business: we had to do all of this as gently as possible, so as not to dislodge the cocoons from where they'd fixed to the lid. We had to remove any remaining wisps of silk, which would prevent the butterflies from being able to emerge. Nia gripped the edge of the lid, and she and Sam moved it together, slowly, so slowly, into the waiting holder.

The next day, one chrysalis began to leak. The fluid was red, but not exactly blood-like; it was thinner, more orange. It looked vegetal, not animal.

While we slept, they emerged. And in the morning, there they were: five new creatures. Their wings were not yet open. They clung to the edges of their house, their feelers flinching. Nia tried to touch the furry undersides of their bodies through the pores of the netting.

We need to stay quiet, Sam said, for the next day or so. And we need to feed them.

We cut up an overripe nectarine, sopping with juice, and deposited it in the bottom of the house.

One afternoon, Nia and I went outside to meet with another person. We were allowed now to meet with one person from another household if we kept our distance. We met my mum, whom we had not seen for months. I spoke to Nia sternly ahead of the meeting. I paced out two metres. We sat at the edge of the river and Nia collected flowers, and at first she seemed to enjoy the game of keeping her distance. Getting so close but no closer, throwing things towards her nan, who stayed seated on a bench. But as she began to tire, Nia edged closer and closer, and I had to keep telling her to move back. To be more careful. I drew an imaginary circle around my mum again. Nia grew sullen. When will the germs be gone? Nia said. When can we play again, Nana? My mum and I looked at each other. Soon, I hope, my mum said. And then Nia said, Can we go home now?

When we got back to the flat, the butterflies were opening their wings, flexing them slowly and experimentally. Painted ladies. The chrysalises were shredded on the holder. One had disappeared entirely, but the others hung there still, torn and translucent, like discarded prophylactics. There was no sign of the gold. Just a bright stain of red left behind on the lid where the liquid had seeped out. We squatted at the side of the butterfly house and watched. One of the creatures fluttered down onto the fruit. It used its long, thin legs to explore, and a proboscis instead of a mouth. Nothing of the caterpillar seemed to remain in the creature's dusty wings and body. Nia tried to stroke one through the gauze of the net again.

Careful, Sam said.

Be gentle, I said.

We left Nia crouched over the butterflies and we went to make tea. When I came back through, the butterfly house was on its side in the middle of the room. Nia was hitting the netting and her hands were bouncing off it. The creatures inside were a blur of movement.

Nia, what are you doing? I shouted. Nia?

Nia went still. She stared at the butterfly house and dropped her fists.

I put her to bed crying. She had cried for over an hour, and was gasping, still, as she fell asleep. *I just wanted to feel them flying*, she had said, between sobs.

Sam and I argued later about what we should do about Nia's behaviour. Sam thought we should punish her for hurting the butterflies. That she needed to learn the importance of being gentle. I didn't know what we should do—except surely not that.

I had recently heard a story on the radio about a girl in Vietnam who had loved a duck so much it had made her ill—all the stories on the radio were about viruses and police killings now. The girl had brought the duck into her home, made a pet of it, and when it died, her brother buried it and then she dug it back up to bury it again. She loved its body, she touched the dead duck so much, that the virus that lived there passed on to her. She had gotten sick and gone to the hospital and a doctor listened to her and knew that she must have avian flu and treated her, and the child lived and grew strong. This story was presented as though we could learn something from it. I thought there must be some kind of lesson for me and Sam and Nia in it. But when I told Sam the story, I couldn't end it properly. I couldn't make any lesson appear.

I didn't see the old man go. But one night, when I looked for him, the bed was empty. The light was still on. The porcelain cats were still there, looking out implacably over the space in which he had lain.

A yellow van from a charity came to collect his furniture. An estate agent came and dressed the house, removing all the porcelain cats and replacing them with lamps and pictures. The house sold quickly.

We took the butterflies down to the river. The white blossom had come in, and there was a gluey smell of newness. We opened the roof of their house. For a while, the butterflies didn't really move. They flinched their antennae back and forth. Then one began to flutter. It fluttered up and out of the house and briefly touched Nia. It landed right on her hand in the manner of a fairy tale or a wish. She was convulsed with delight.

It tickled me, Mama, it tickled me. Did you see?

One by one, the others emerged too, landing briefly on surfaces close-by—a dock-leaf, Sam's shoe—before rising up and fluttering into the trees and out of sight.

That evening, at bedtime, Nia asked me what would happen next to the caterpillars. She was lying in my arms after her story.

I reminded her that they were butterflies now, that they had reached the final stage of the life cycle.

But what then? What does *final stage* mean? she asked. What do they become next?

She kept pressing, and eventually I said: Well, then they'll die. They'll become dust, and maybe sludge, and the whole cycle will start again.

She was quiet for a while. Then she asked, Mama, do people die? Or is it only butterflies?

I once believed that if I had a child, the fundamental processes of life and death might become clearer to me. But even the basic tenets of biology now escape me.

One of the difficulties of establishing whether there's life on other planets is that there's no agreed definition of life. I read that somewhere.

What could I say to Nia about any of this?

I told her that people go back to the earth when they die.

She looked bewildered.

So was I in the ground before I was a baby? she asked.

No, I said. Not exactly. Once, you were a tiny egg inside me. And after you die, you go back to being something... different.

Nia was concentrating hard on my words, so much so that she was scowling.

So I was really small inside you, she said, and then I got big, and then I'll be really small again?

Sort of, I said. But... it's more like you become something different.

Do people grow back again then? she asked. Like plants? And then: When will *I* die, Mama?

And I had to stop myself from this lie—I wanted so much to believe in this lie: Never, never, never.

Lovebirds

Three weeks after Emile moved in, I came home from my shift to find him in the dark in his underpants. He was wearing the stethoscope he'd bought for a fancy-dress party and was settling its drum against the living-room wall.

Shhhh, he said. The neighbours are doing something *really weird.*

The neighbours? I said. Yeah, the neighbours are the weird ones alright.

When I turned on the lights, Emile peeled himself away, leaving a slick print of his torso on the pale green paint.

There were other signs. His shifts dwindled to nothing and he smoked all day long. When we went out, he thought people were watching him. When we stayed in, he thought people were ignoring him. He said he had dreams that I would leave him and he baked bread in the shape of my name. He bought me terrible gifts with all of his Universal Credit.

The last straw was the parrot.

But you love birds! he said. You've always loved birds!

The parrot had a bright pink face and a bright green body, and though we never knew its sex, he called it Lillian. The creature strutted along the sofa and shat on my work bag.

Emile talked to Lillian constantly, but she never learned

to speak. She took chunks out of the furniture and began to pluck out her own feathers. Sometimes she flew in a rage at the gaudy reflection in the mirror. She went berserk when anyone visited.

One night, when I stepped into the flat after work, she went straight for me and drew blood from my cheek.

That's it, I said, we can't keep her cooped up any more. It's cruel.

I strode over to the window of our flat and opened it.

Lillian fluttered over and sat on the ledge, ticking her head from left to right.

Don't, Emile said. Please. She was expensive. Just shut the window.

I paused for a moment and the warm air rushed in, wild and inviting against my skin. The bird looked at me with black glass eyes. She cocked her head, as though listening carefully to the world outside. And she made no sound but suddenly she swooped out and down, and quickly became indistinguishable from the sky.

A low cry began to rise. Emile was keening, moving from foot to foot, ticking from left to right.

What am I going to do now? he said. What am I going to do now?

Later that night we leaned out of the window together, smoking cigarettes, scanning the glittering horizon. We'd talked it through. Emile was going to get help. I would go with him the next morning.

We imagined Lillian out in the dark, fluttering up from the trees at the edge of the park, beginning to discover the extent of the city.

There. There. Do you think that's her? Right there?

What if she's lonely out there? Emile said.

She was lonely in here, I said.

I'd heard stories of brightly coloured birds being mobbed by crows and magpies.

But also, I'd heard that flocks of feral parakeets thrived noisily in the trees of suburbia. Emile once told me that Jimi Hendrix loved birds and released a pair of parakeets on Carnaby Street—that their descendants still flew wild over the capital. The supposedly grey streets of Manchester are home to gaudy cherry blossom and coconut-ice magnolia, to brick-red foxes and butterflies whose wings are acid blue. Why not to our Lil as well? She'll be a neon blur on the roof of a warehouse; she'll be a shuttlecock of malice and colour above us in the sky.

The mouth of vault

I hooked up with Death at the Christmas Market. We'd been flirting for a while online. He'd gone under the name *Death_by_Proxy*, but he really was called Death—or, more precisely, Matthew De'Ath.

When we met, I asked if I could still call him Death. I've gotten used to it, I said.

If you must, he replied.

I got smashed on mulled wine and Death stayed sober. A bright, cold moon hung in the sky above us. Death said very little. He rolled beautiful cigarettes, lining them up on the table in front of us. He had blond hair that he wore in curtains, and his neck was finely muscled. When he spoke, the tendons there flexed, as though he was bracing against each interaction. He was thirty-two, according to his profile—almost a decade older than me.

You're drunk, he said, as the cold tightened in around us. I'll drive you home.

So I followed Death through the backstreets of Chinatown to his car—a decrepit Polo he'd left in a cheap car park.

You shouldn't let strangers drive you out here, he said, when we were out on the moortops in his tin can.

Not in this kind of car I shouldn't, I said.

I asked him to pull up and then we kissed for a long time. There was the faintest light still at the horizon, a watermark of pink over Saddleworth Moor.

He stopped kissing me.

You ok? I said.

I think we should wait, he said.

Wait? I said. Wait for what?

He looked away.

I can fuck you now, if that's what you really want, Death said. But I'd prefer to wait. I think it's going to snow.

Amina, my flatmate, was furious when I got in. I was drunk, horny, already making plans to see him again.

You *drove* home with him? she said. Libby, you've got to stop doing this.

Well, I said, I googled him. He checks out. He's even got a LinkedIn, with his place of work listed. Would a serial killer get away with being called Death?

Double bluff, she said. And then she made us tea, and we sat together in my bed and she asked me to recount every little detail.

I'd been seeing Death for six months when he suggested we take a trip together.

I could show you where I grew up, if you want, he said, in his diffident way.

We were hanging out most weekends by then. I'd drag Death to late bars. I'd dance and Death would watch me. He rarely started conversations, but when he did, it was to impart information, for instance, to tell me about the discography of Roots Manuva and the observer effect in quantum physics—the way that looking at an object emits a tiny bit of light, which changes the object you're trying to look at. He revealed only informational biographical details about himself. He'd moved to Manchester with his sister when he was just a teenager, but he'd been born in Norfolk. When I asked him what it was like there, he told me nothing about his school, or his friends, or his early memories. Instead, he gave me a history lesson on agricultural work in the region and told me that his grandfather had arrived in the county with five children and all his worldly goods piled on a cart.

I liked being driven places by Death, so when he suggested the trip I said, Yeah, sure, why not? It'll be almost like we're *a couple*.

We drove west to east—from Manchester, across the Peak District, down through Lincolnshire and then into Norfolk. I'd made us a playlist and I downed cans of cocktails in the passenger seat. The big skies and the big green streamed past us at speed. After King's Lynn, the roads began to narrow. Great bales of hay were rolled up in the fields around us. I spy with my little eye, W for windmill. Back there, no there, over that fucking hedge. Death wouldn't look away from the road for even a second. R is for roadkill. More and more of it as we got deeper into Norfolk—big things too, things you'd really feel as you hit them. Two game birds, partially flattened. Rabbits. A badger slumped at the side of the road. We drove through villages of redbrick cottages. Handwritten signs in front gardens offered us Homemade Jam and Pickles and Marmalade and New Potatoes. We turned onto a single-track road and three pheasants stumbled out from the hedgerow, one after the other, then wobbled along the tarmac. Implausible, gobbling creatures.

It's the hottest August bank holiday on record and the cottage we are staying in has an Aga and two-foot-thick stone walls. It must once have been an agricultural store house. Low ceilings, small rooms, tiny windows. We both have to duck at each doorway. There's a staircase so steep that I go up to see the bedroom on all fours. There's no phone reception. The Wi-Fi's sketchy to non-existent.

Shall we go to the sea? I say. Right now?

Alright, Death says.

We get back in the car and drive. Past neatly farmed fields and a brewery and rows of workers' cottages painted in cheerful holiday colours.

We park up at the edge of woodland.

Where is it then? I say. This beach?

The beach is about a mile away, he says. There's the woods, then the freshwater marsh, then the saltwater marsh, and then the beach.

Christ, I say. I'll vaporise in this heat.

We walk through the woodland, sun dappling the long stretch of purple sea lavender that runs alongside the path. We reach a boardwalk that extends out over the marshes. There's no one else here. I follow Death onto the suspended wooden platform, my footsteps echoing his. It's almost evening now, though the heat is still intense. There's a slight breeze here at least, which must be coming off the sea though I still can't see it—the long, flat marshes hide the future from us. I catch a glimpse of a boat suspended in the tall grass up ahead—so the ocean must really be there. There's a low electrical buzz of insects in the undergrowth. A shimmer of a breeze through the rushes.

When the boardwalk runs out, the sea is finally in view—just. A distant ribbon of blue between the sand dunes. It must be another mile out at least.

This is nothing like the seaside that I know from childhood drives through busy towns, the ice-cream stalls and rock shops and flipflop vendors ushering you in, the beach spilling out ahead of you, the sea and the day-trippers and the hot doughnut sugar hazing on the horizon just as you taste the salt on your tongue.

Still more walking, I groan.

Are we nearly there yet, Death mimics.

The first part of the beach is smashed razor shells. But then it's fine white-gold sand, and we kick off our shoes and it's burning hot on the soles of our feet.

There isn't another soul in sight. There are small white jellyfish and long clumps of glassy seaweed. There's a great roaring in the sky—a fly-over of military planes, loud and low.

You coming in then? says Death. He strips, straightforwardly, and folds his clothes into a pile.

I peel off my dress and I follow him. It's shallow for a long way, and breathtakingly cold for the first few deep paces. Then it's glorious. I lean back and float. Dazzling sun. Salt on my lips.

Death dives under the water and disappears.

Death? I shout. Come back, you unit.

Nothing. Nothing. Roar of the planes overhead. Then more nothing.

No one else here. The shoosh of the sea. The shoosh of the breeze running all the way back to the salt marsh.

Death? I shout. Stop fucking about.

He surfaces a way away.

Come here, he says.

And when I do, he licks the salt from my lips. His cold-sea mouth is electricity in my ear, on my shoulder, up the ridges of my throat.

We drive back inland. We eat chips outside a pub and suck the vinegar from our fingertips. A row of salmon-pink cottages stands across the road, a line of tall tissue-paper flowers in front of them in pastel colours, somehow surviving the sea air. We walk to them, so I can take a picture that I'll never upload, and they stand taller even than Death.

Behind the cottages, small boats are tethered here and there on wet sand. But we can't get far, walking. We're stymied at each turn by new inlets.

It's coming in around us, Death says.

But the sea looks so far away again—miles out on the horizon.

The cottage is boiling hot when we return. We open all of the small windows, but the darkness outside is hot too. There are no human sounds out here. The village is three miles away. The night is not quiet though. There are alien noises out there in the fields.

What is that? I ask Death.

Pheasants, he says. Noisy buggers.

When I open the last window latch, two small moths briefly distinguish themselves from the woodwork, then find a new place to hide.

We climb up the stairs on all fours. We remind each other to duck through the doorway. When the lights are out, we listen to an owl close by. No twit, it's all wo-oo-oo, a jabbering, fussy, grief-stricken sound.

Death fucks me in a blind, close, missionary way.

Afterwards I say: That was a bit like being buried alive, wasn't it? Or maybe like being married?

He says: You know what, Lib? You don't need to say everything you're thinking out loud.

Listen, I say. I need to pee, and I'm not going back down there on my own.

You really are an infant, Death says.

I make him sing a song for me at the bathroom door.

Death, I say, you're *really bad* at singing. To humiliate yourself like this, I think you must be in love with me.

He laughs. Or coughs, maybe. That's what you think, is it?

The next morning, we walk to the village. This is the village where Death grew up. Though it's hardly a village, to my mind; there's no pub, for a start—just a cluster of old cottages, a cul-de-sac of new-build houses, and a church.

Isn't this more of a hamlet? I say, knowing Death likes to talk about categories like this.

No, he says. First off, a hamlet doesn't have a church. And also, more people live here than you'd think. The old bakehouse, that's, like, five separate flats. There, that's where we lived.

He points to a small, dark cottage whose front door opens right into the road.

Okay, I say. It just seems more like a... street than a village.

The church sits on a small hillock behind the cottages and is called Our Lady St Mary. We pace the rows of gravestones. The names here are weird: Shackcloth. Makins. Yarham. Church. Purple. Sexton. Edge. Tann. Pond. Grief. Crisp.

Twite. Pilch. Meek. Meek. Meek. Fluck. Bright. Grimes. Pope—Lazarus Pope. And yes, Death.

There they are, Death says. My grandparents.

William De'Ath

Lydia De'Ath

Okay, I say. Nice to meet you, Wills and Lyds.

I don't remember them, Death says. Not really.

Oh, I say. And then, because it's awkward, and what do you say at a graveside, I tell him a story about my nan, who I lived with for a while, and who loved me very much, but she showed that love by cooking me things that I found disgusting: tripe with vinegar and pigs' trotters stew and dumplings that were never cooked through. So I made excuses not to eat with her, and then when she died, I wanted all of it back—even the chewy white tripe and the condensed milk and the stewed kidneys. Death looks at me for a long time after I've said all this, and then he walks off.

There is a large, poorly constructed door affixed to the church porch. It's made of wood and wire mesh. A sign attached to it reads: *Please keep this door closed to protect Our Lady from squirrels*. Inside, the church is in a poor condition. Damp plasterwork and mould. It's a simple chapel: leaded windows, but no stained glass. The old beams and the high ceiling and the stone walls are white-washed. The only decorations are embroidered banners and a ghoulish sculpture of St Edmund that looks like it's made of papier mâché. There are flagstones under our feet marked with the names and dates of clergymen. One stone, the largest one, bears the chiselled inscription: *The Mouth of Vault.*

The Mouth of Vault. What does that mean? I ask Death.

What do you mean, what does it mean? he says. There's a vault under our feet.

But, it's so... occult sounding, I say. *The Mouth of Vault.* Is it an ecclesiastical thing? Like, something from Revelation?

No, he says. It's just a place designation.

Why just one definite article then? Why not *The mouth of the vault*? I say. It's definitely occult. It's like saying, The Neck of Womb. Like, just call it the cervix anyway, if you're not trying to creep people out. What I'm saying is, just call it a fucking door if it's not... occult.

Don't you ever stop? Death says.

Later, we pull up to a cottage on the roadside and he buys samphire and fresh eggs and cream. I watch him talking to the woman at her door. He looks more relaxed than usual, talking to her—big, handsome, sun-scorched. Death says he'll cook for us. He's good at that. He regularly makes meals using more than three ingredients. So, when evening falls, he makes us a carbonara and I mix us some drinks. Afterwards, we sit outside the cottage, on the banking at the edge of the road. The stars are glinting above us. More and more of them, the more you look—the sky seeming to speed away from us in these points of light.

Death starts listing constellations. Ursa Minor, just there, he says. And next to it, there, to the left, Cepheus. Capella. Perseus. My dad taught me them, he says.

There's no point telling me what they're called, I say. I'll never remember the names. Do you want to fuck me? Out here? There's no one to see us.

No, Death says. I don't. I was trying to... talk to you.

Oh, te-di-ous, I say.

He turns to look at me then. He puts his big hand over my face. Then he stands up.

Oh, God, I say. You're upset. Death, come back and tell me about the stars then...

But he's turned away from me. He's stalking back into the cottage.

I get up and follow him. I catch him in the hallway. There are two moths dancing round the low light bulb.

Look, I say. I'm sorry.

Are you? He says. It's only ever really about you, isn't it, Lib?

He pulls away then. He turns with magnificent purpose, his head still turning as he tries to walk away from me.

I don't tell him to duck. I stand there, watching, and I don't tell him to duck.

His head hits the doorframe to the kitchen at a bad angle. He turns right into the impact, so that he headbutts the stone with the very top of his skull.

Death falls forwards, onto his knees.

I can't move, though I have the instinct to turn away from him. I feel like I'm watching something intimate unfold, something he wouldn't want me to see. There's a tremor rising in my belly. I feel like I might laugh.

Death groans. He's on his hands and knees now. He crawls a little way into the kitchen. I follow him. There is a bright, neat, line of blood running down his forehead.

Shit, I say. Shit. Are you ok?

Fuck, he says. And then he groans again. Yeah, yeah, I'm alright.

I'll get you a cloth, I say, and I run to the bathroom—ducking at the doorway—and I soak a white flannel in hot water.

When I come back, he's sitting on the floor with his head hanging downwards. He looks drunk.

I kneel down next to him. I wipe the blood from his forehead. Then I part his hair to try to see where it's coming from.

Fuck, he says, right off.

Sorry, I say. I'm just trying to see what's... going on.

I'm nauseated doing this, but I carry on. I push his hair to one side. It's bad under here. There's a wide section that's welling with blood—where all of the skin has been razed away by the stone doorframe. I take the wet cloth and just sort of spread it over the whole of his head. It soaks through quickly—so red. When I take the cloth away, there's a shimmering jelly forming where there was once a scalp.

I'm just, I say, I'm just going to get a new cloth.

In the bathroom, I run water in the sink and rinse the cloth out and I panic. There's no phone reception. I can't drive. I can't fucking drive. He's right: I am an infant. If he passes out, how will I be able to get him anywhere? Death is enormous. And the village is three miles away. Would I even be able to find my way back there?

Calm down. Calm yourself the fuck down. It's a superficial wound. There are no arteries in the top of your head, right? It looks bad, but he's not going to bleed out.

I go back to the kitchen with another cloth. He's still sitting there on the stone floor.

I felt a bit weird for a moment, he says. But I'm alright. He's starting to rock forwards, as though he might be about to try to stand.

Don't, I say. I kneel down next to him again. Death, look, maybe you shouldn't move around?

He turns directly to look at me. There's blood running round his hairline. There's blood running down the edge of one of his ears.

You do know, don't you, that my name isn't actually Death? My name is Matthew.

Please, I say, don't move.

He staggers up. Stands there for a moment.

I get up too.

I should have stayed close to him. I should have propped him up. I should have led him by the arm to a seat.

Instead, I back away. He's roiling on the spot like a boxer about to go down.

Why don't we just sit down over here? I say. Royal we. But I'm moving even further away from him.

Why don't we...? he says. Why don't we just...?

There's blood running down his face. There's blood running into his mouth.

He stumbles forwards, and then he goes again. This time he falls like a felled tree, his forehead hitting hard against the other side of the same stone doorframe. This time there's a crack like the sound of an axe as it splits wood clean apart.

Death_by_Proxy. Looking for: Casual fun/ Something more/ A relationship. His profile's still up. He never deactivated it. The picture of him is black and white. He looks downwards, away from the camera. He's smiling and moving his hair to the side with one hand. His forehead is clean and smooth. Sometimes I look at his LinkedIn. Sometimes at his FB page—one profile picture, the info only half-populated. I couldn't even name a next of kin. When I look at his pages, I remember that slab in the church. The Mouth of Vault. And the dark activity behind the interface: html coding, the soft palate hardening, the way you alter something when you try to look at it. There are stars, overhead. Constellations whose names I cannot remember. Matthew, he said to me. My name is Matthew.

Intermittent visual disturbances

All that winter the sun was low on the horizon and dazzlingly bright. She would turn a corner in the city—the streets of which she walked for hours each day—and a sudden slice of light would blind her for several steps before the light dropped once more below the level of the built-up horizon. All that winter long she had a low-level headache, like a band of metal was being slowly tightened around her skull, and the world began to shimmer ahead of her.

How do you live? was the question she asked of the people she met that winter, though she could never have asked it directly. Instead, she listened in to strangers' conversations for clues. As she sits in the doctor's surgery clutching the note she has written in case of dumb crying (*Relapse—Unable to work or sleep—Intermittent visual disturbances—Progressively higher dose, please*), and as she stands in the queue in the pharmacy, she listens, willing people to reveal their way of living to her.

She goes to stay with her father for Christmas. He has his own problems and lives in a caravan on a piece of land that he will never have the money to build on. He has been married three times and now only has her, this sorry daughter, and his caravan to show for it. She watches him measure out his pleasures. One glass of warm ale each evening. A film that has been given to him on a memory stick by someone in the pub. A road trip in the planning with his brother across to the west coast of Scotland.

For New Year, she goes to stay with Taz, an old friend who practises meditation each morning and evening. The bedsit smells of citrus, and Taz drinks flower teas all day long and is applying for jobs abroad and seems hopeful, though she has no regular work and no contact with her family. When the medication makes her grind her teeth and shiver, Taz makes her cups of tea and wraps her up in blankets.

In the mercilessly bright days of February, she goes to stay with her cousin, Julia. She arrives on Julia's doorstep with no warning. Her cousin lets her share her clothes and her toothbrush and her bed. No questions are asked. In the night, her cousin cries in her sleep because she is in so much pain—and the crying doesn't wake her up because she is used to being in so much pain. In the morning, Julia takes a host of pills and waits for them to take effect. There are always people staying with Julia, friends who are sick or homeless or are going cold-turkey or have taken abortion pills and need somewhere away from their children to bleed and be cared for. Julia plans meals for them and remembers wild and happy things they have done together and writes lists of things for her to try to do each day.

When she returns home to Grove House, she sees that everywhere, in every direction, worse things by far are happening to other people.

That thought is almost obliterating.

And also: in every direction, she sees what they are doing to live. She makes herself see it.

Her neighbour, Jan, had to identify her son's body, and she has found a way—she plants the communal garden with bulbs in the coldest months, using a little cushion for her knees, and she pushes mobiles that spin in the breeze into the earth along with gnomes and porcelain fairies for the children who live in their block to discover. One neighbour complains that the gnomes are ugly, but Jan does not relent.

Stevie on the top deck goes down to the river each day and picks up litter that collects in the rushes and he fishes with magnets for scrap that he will take to sell or keep in his flat if he finds it sufficiently unusual or interesting.

Nadia has recently moved onto her floor with her three children, but Nadia is not her real name; she has had to leave everything behind her, including that. Nadia fills the windows of her flat with paper lanterns and fairy lights, which she leaves on all through the night. She knocked on all the neighbours' doors with her children to wish them a happy new year.

One day the spring arrives, suddenly, like this: a tree on the street illuminated in the early sun, the new buds at the ends of its branches glistening there. It is awfully bright. But she looks straight at it and her line of sight does not waver.

Sour Hall

An old butter churn, the wood waxy and black; a cattle shed with great gaps in the roof; and a vicious white horse called Mary—these are the things that we inherit along with the house. George isn't one for superstitions or bad omens. She says we'll start again and make the farm ours. She says we'll make something better of it than her old man ever did.

She's hired a box van and we sit high up in the cab either side of Shaun, our extra muscle. We drive the steep, narrow road up the valley side, judder across a cattle grid, and then we're onto the long road that slices across the moortops. Our turning is marked by a sign at knee height: *Sour Hall Farm*, it reads, the words mouldered with wood rot. This road isn't tarmacked, and cobbles and building-rubble fill the worst of the pits, in an attempt to make it passable. The van bounces then grounds, a horrible sound of metal on rock. George hits the accelerator.

Steady on, Georgie, Shaun says. I paid the deposit on this van for you, you know.

It is late summer. The sky over the farm is hazed with yellow, the hills around us drenched in gold.

George parks the van alongside the house, behind an old

Land Rover she's bought off eBay. She jumps down from the cab, runs to open the passenger door for me.

What do you think? she says.

I've only visited once before. Sour Hall passed to George last year, but we waited for the weather to turn to make a start on the building work. The front of the house has been painted and fettled: gutters fixed, window frames repaired, the old stonework coated with adhesive to stop the wind and the rain driving in through the winter—even through two feet of wall, the rain had turned the plasterwork inside black with mould. Above the door, the numbers 1684 are scored in deep, though George says the house has burned down at least twice in its history, so that stone might be the only thing that old that still remains.

It looks smart, I say. It looks dead smart.

Inside, George has been relentless. When we first visited, the house was dark and cluttered and smelled of teabags and manure. She's gutted it. She shows me the new kitchen, the new bathroom, the bedrooms that have been re-plastered, re-wired and freshly painted. She shows me the old utility room, which is now a workspace where she'll process orders. Each room is clean and bright and smells of volatile chemicals. Nothing of her parents remains.

I'm going to start on the boxes, Shaun shouts through to us.

Let me show you the shed, George says, and she's practically dancing me back outside. This is her real pride. This is where most of the money's gone, the EU development grant that she won to restore the dairy. She hadn't seen her parents for more than twenty years before her mother, and then her father, went, in quick succession. But George's father left all of the information she needed in shoe boxes on the kitchen table: bills, letters of sale, old advertisements—evidence of Sour Hall farm serving the Calder Valley since the seventeenth century. He left her this, and the paperwork for the grant, all ready to be completed. But George isn't exactly grateful. She has no fond memories, she says, of him nor of the old farm. *It's ours now, not his*, she says. *It's our hard work that'll pay us off. We've nowt to be grateful for.*

We walk into the milking shed together. The roof has been patched up—no raw scraps of sky above us now. The wooden beams have been repaired, light new oak patching into the old timbers, which are black from the fire that put George's father finally out of business. There are pens for the cows, who'll need to stay in during the winter months when the grass is poor and the weather would perish the fat and the milk from them. There is hay baled out and waiting for milking time, and already a hint of the warm, green smell of their urine, of the soft cud at their lips.

Just through here to the new dairy, George says.

The room at the far end of the barn—a dingy old shed the last time I visited—has been completely refurbished. It's immaculately white now and forensically clean. It houses steel vats and steel storage containers and steel fridges for the milk. There's a cold current in here.

Fridges on already? I ask.

George smiles. There are dimples in the reddish flesh of her cheeks. She looks as though she's already a farmer. Not yet, she says. You'll get used to the moors, Ashleigh love, and that east wind.

She shows me the electronic churn and the sachets of blue and white mould cultures and the gleaming surfaces where she'll knead salt into the fresh butter.

It's on the way out that I spot it, the one old thing that George has kept: the ancient butter churn that we found out here when we first visited. An old, blackened anomaly, squatting in the corner of the dairy.

George sees me looking. You need some wood in the environment, she says. Something old and damp to stop the air from drying out. She looks around the room then as though searching for snags, for something left undone.

I'll need to keep the bacterial levels consistent in here. It's a delicate business, you know, she says, as she closes the door behind us. You won't need to come into the dairy, Ash, once we get going.

We spend the afternoon shifting furniture and boxes inside the house. Then we sit out on the grass with Shaun and he rolls a ciggie and George vapes, making big icing-sugar clouds on the air. Even now, even at the deepest, warmest point of summer, the wind is wild up here and we clutch our jackets around us.

You girls really going to be alright out here? Shaun says. He trains his eyes out on the moorland horizon. There's rural crime, you know, plenty of it, he says. Lads out after cattle and cars and equipment.

George gives me a look. Ta for the tip, Shaun, she says. I've never been to the countryside before. I didn't grow up out here or owt, so that's right useful.

Just saying, Shaun says. You could do with a gun, George. Or some dogs at the very least.

I can take care of us, don't you worry, George says.

Shaun grinds his cig into the ground. He needs to get the van back to Manchester.

Once he's gone, George and I put on jumpers and sit outside until the hills darken and the colour burns out of the sky.

I'll dig us a fire pit, George says. I'll dig it tomorrow! She kisses my fingers until they're warm.

I feel it before I hear it: a sharp bang that cracks through the bones of my spine.

Ashleigh, love, George says, laughing, cupping her warm hand to the nape of my neck. You jumped a mile. It's just a gate somewhere, banging closed. The wind up here makes sounds travel all over. You'll hear a sheep bleat from miles away, as though it's in the field right next to you. You'll get used to it, Ash. There's nowt up here can hurt us.

The cows arrive a week later. The transporter can't make it up the steep, narrow road to Sour Hall, so George borrows a horse box from a couple who farm across the valley and brings the Friesians up one at a time. Unloading each of them is an act of devotion for her. She stands in the field at the bottom of the ramp, lowing. The very first one refuses to budge. George mounts the box, pats the cow's thick neck as though she's a dog, murmurs something into her whiskered ear. Then she leads her down, shoulder to shoulder, and the cow trots out into the field, lifting her muzzle, braying at us. She stalks around the perimeter, then begins to run along it.

What's she doing? I ask. I thought cows were docile?

She's after the others, George says. They don't like to be alone. Let's get them shifted quick as we can.

After the Friesians, we take delivery of the Ayrshires and then the Red Poll. All of them dairy cattle. All of them big, solid creatures. They've muscled flanks, but their hips protrude like coat-hangers as they walk. We'll milk them twice a day with the shiny new equipment, the clusters in various shapes and sizes that fasten to the cows, cool steel sucking at their warm bodies. George will make organic cheese and organic cheese-custards and raw, fermented butters for fancy restaurants in Manchester. She'll sell in the local farmers' markets too. She has grand plans for an online shop, for contracts with Morrisons and the local Co-op. The cows will calve each year, and we'll keep some of the females to slowly grow the herd.

What about bull calves? I ask one evening. What will we do with the bull calves?

George is taking her boots off. She's just come in from checking on the pregnant cow, Vera, and on the dairy, where our first vat of milk is fermenting.

I've been thinking, she says, of keeping them. For a bit, at least. Now folk don't want veal, most farmers shoot the bull calves at birth, or freight them to the Continent. Just as cruel, if you ask me, the mothers full of milk and wanting to feed their young.

George looks up at me, carefully. She comes and stands close by, rubs the back of my neck like she's started doing with her favourite Ayrshire, Margery.

We wouldn't do it how it used to be done, she says. We'd feed the calves properly, let them suckle for a good few months. So the girls'll get to mother them for a bit. And we could sell the meat, when it's time. Rose veal, it's called, when they've been given the chance to grow and roam. Pink it is, not like that pale, white meat when they've not been fed right. What do you think?

I nod. But my chest feels tight. Vera, the long-lashed Red who likes to lick my boots, is growing bigger and bigger.

She'll calf in late spring. I will not think about it. I do not think about it.

When the sun goes down here, the night's thick as stout. I sleep fitfully, startling awake over and over, a muffled echo of something bang, bang, banging in my ears.

We're used to hard work. George has looked after herself since she left the farm at sixteen. For the last two decades, she's worked in factories and in warehouses and on building sites. She's done deliveries, driving up and down the M62 in sixteen-hour shifts. She's emptied slot-machines and shifted pianos and washing machines and double beds. I've worked in kitchens and hotels and pubs, changing barrels, pulling pints, clearing tables, grafting into the small hours for more than a decade now. We're used to working until our bodies ache and our thoughts are blunted.

You up to this, my love? George asked me, when we first met. We were in the back room of The Swan with Two Necks, George's last pub. I'd fetched up looking for work, and the job came with the offer of accommodation, which I needed badly.

This isn't an easy job, she said. You'll get all kinds of bother. And the regulars will try it on. I mean, really try it on.

I've worked all over, I said. I've worked bars in Rochdale and Salford and Liverpool. I'm a grafter. I can take care of myself.

Is that right? she said, not unkindly. She was studying my face—the swollen purple of my eyes that concealer couldn't mask. My hair was shorter than it had been a week before, levelled off by my sister with a pair of kitchen scissors.

I'll give you a week's trial, she said.

I've been with her ever since. We're both used to hard work, we are, but by the end of October we're knackered.

The weather's turned and our lips are chapped. We ache all over from the graft—our joints grind and we find new points of tenderness in our shoulder blades, our knees, the knuckle-bones of our necks. My ears ring from the constant wind. We scrub up all the time, lathering up to our elbows to keep the milk clean. George's thumbs both split open and my nails start to peel away in soft white layers.

George looks for help with the evening milking. When the men arrive, they park up on the moor and walk down to the house in a style that I can't read. They're leisurely, they will not be rushed. But they are not relaxed. Theirs is not an amiable gait. There are three of them, and the eldest knew George's father. *Georgina*, he keeps calling her as we walk around the farm, and she clatters about, slamming gates, kicking buckets, trying to murder the sound of the old name.

After they've had a good look around, we sit in the kitchen and George brings them beers.

You missed a lot, Georgina, the older one says. He fills her in on local scandals: the horse-meat butchered in the valley and working its way into supermarket lasagnes. The old sisters who used to farm up at Slack whose front door was eaten away by badgers, finally alerting folk to their deaths. He tells her about foot and mouth, about the animal carcasses piled in fields around the valley, quick-limed in mass graves while farmers wept. And he tells her about the last fire at Sour Hall. There's real relish in his voice then, as he tells her how her father was put in hospital, how his lungs were ruined by smoke as he tried to get his cows out.

Lucky he weren't stamped to death, he says. It's the boggart, tha knows.

The two lads snigger and shake their heads.

You can laugh, he says, but Georgina knows. He tried to leave Sour Hall, her father, but that boggart wouldn't have it.

George looks in my direction now. She winks at me.

Peter, she says, you've had too much ale.

'Appen you're right, he says. Is that old horse, Mary, still around?

Can I use your lav? one of the lads asks, and George points him upstairs.

The cows are braying at something outside; several of them calling loud and low at once.

I'll go up, I say, and have a look out over the fields.

When I get to the top of the stairs, the lad is standing with the bathroom door open, pissing into the toilet. He turns round to look at me, still holding his cock. He doesn't say anything, but he smiles at me, slow and wolfish. He shakes his cock, puts it away, wipes his hands on his jeans, and then walks out onto the landing. When he gets close to me, I flinch. And then he laughs and jogs away down the stairs.

Why did I stop? Why did I give him that chance to laugh? I turn into our bedroom and I hit the back of the door with the ball of my fist. I'm stupid. I'm so stupid. I let it happen, I let it happen, I always just let it happen. I hit the door again, bang, bang, banging it until the flesh of my palms starts to throb.

Ashleigh? It's George's voice. Everything alright up there?

I move to the window, to do what I was meant to: look out on the cows. They're charging across the field, running downhill, away from the milking shed.

Something's spooked the girls, I shout. You'd best go to the field.

*

I don't like them, I tell George later on.

It's dark outside now and she's come back in, carrying the cold inside with her. I'm washing up and her cheek is a scrap of night sky against my neck.

There'd been no sign of what had frit the girls, but George and the men had found them bunched together at the far end of the field. One of them had hurt her leg in the stampede. *You can start now*, George had told the two young ones. *Help me get this lot back up for milking.*

They're harmless, she says. They're just lads.

I tell her about the pissing one. She laughs out loud. Then she sees my face and stops.

Look, he was probably embarrassed, trying to style it out. You know what lads are like. Don't go soft on me, Ashleigh. If you really don't like them after a few weeks, I'll find someone else.

She fastens her arms around me. She moves her mouth into my hair, nuzzles across the back of my neck, her lips still cold.

Let's go to bed, she says.

At the start of November, the first frost sets across the moor—a hard, dazzling white. We need to do something about the horse, Mary, before the fields get too hard. We've tried to stable her with the cows, but she bolts at the door. She grazes as far away from us as she can, only eats the hay that we put out for her when we're backed a good distance off. She bucks when we tether her, bares her teeth and shrieks. But she's limping: her feet have overgrown her shoes.

George calls the farrier. He arrives with a van with a chimney, a furnace built-in at the back.

Normally, I charge twenty-five pound for removal and filing, he says, which is a fair price. But I've been up here before, a long while ago. I'll need forty quid to go near her.

We've managed to tether her at the side of the dairy. George and one of the lads brought her up, and now George has a purple crescent of a bruise on her forearm and says she's ready to let the horse go lame and I can talk to the farrier and pay for it myself if I want her seeing to.

Mary's whinnying before we get near her, dancing from side to side.

Easy girl, the farrier says. Normally we'd use a slip knot, he says, presumably for my benefit. So the horse can free hersen if she's distressed. Otherwise they can get hurt trying to escape.

He wears a heavy leather apron, and he fetches from it a long metal file, which he puts on the ground.

That's not going to work with this one, he says. I'll need to fasten her tight.

He ducks under Mary's head, unties the tether and holds her fast. He re-fastens the rope, makes it tighter, so that she's right in against the dairy wall. She bucks from side to side.

I'll be earning my money today, he says.

Mary's head pulls against the rope again and again—like she's viciously nodding. The farrier catches one of her back legs in his hand, bends it up and sets to work immediately. He kicks a metal stool into place, rests the hoof on it, begins to prise out the nails from the shoe. Then he's filing away the hard outgrowth of the hoof. The noise is bad, but he works quickly.

He's on with the second hoof when I hear it: a sharp, loud bang inside the dairy. Mary hears it too. She tries to rear up away from the shed but hits her nose against the wall. She convulses backwards, kicking the stool away. The farrier jumps back, his tools clattering to the ground. Metal clangs around us, carries on clanging around us. Mary's bucking and neighing, her back legs all over the place.

The farrier stands back. We both stand back, just watching. A cold feeling. Panic filling my throat.

Heard the stories about Sour Hall, have you? he asks once everything's gone quiet again.

Maybe, I say. Do you mean about the boggart?

He laughs. The boggart, he says. That's one word for the old bastard. Though George might have some others.

I don't say anything.

Not a talker then? he says. Suit yoursen, but that horse i'nt going to get sorted here.

It takes a while until Mary's calm, but eventually the farrier gets close enough to set her loose. We follow her up to the top field. He catches her there again, does his work.

I'll not come back up here, he says when it's finished. It's not worth my while. I've left her barefoot. She's an old horse. You should set her somewhere with hard ground, and she'll see to hersen until she's done with.

One December afternoon the sky changes colour—it curdles from blue to deep grey. It is bright and dark at the same time, like the light in a man's eyes the moment before he turns on you. The snow falls and falls and obliterates the horizon and then the moor and then our lane. George calls the council, tells them that the road is almost impassable, that our water supply might freeze and then we'll be in real trouble. An hour later we drive out in the Land Rover and see that a snow plough has made it up to the edge of the causeway, has gritted the main road, and then stopped at the neck of our lane and deposited a beaten-up sign, saying *Road Closed*.

We turn back towards home. The car judders as we slide down towards the house. We dig out trenches to the shed so that we can feed the girls. Our hands are raw, our lips are chapped and bleeding. We run the hot water on constant. Will this help? Or will it risk the pipes cracking? We don't know. That night, I smother our fingers with Vaseline and George lies still while I smear it on her lips. The cows are huddled in the shed, their noises muffled in the snow. But I'm sure I can hear it every so often—a dull banging that makes the animals cry out and then go entirely silent.

Christmas and New Year come and go. George buys us good whisky, gives the lads presents. We work together through the longest, darkest nights of the year.

In January my sister calls. Wishes me a happy new year. She doesn't ask after George.

I'm pregnant, she says. And then she says, Sorry.

Don't be sorry, I say. For fuck's sake, don't be sorry. When are you due? Are you ok? Is Paul chuffed?

She's due in May. She's fine but the size of a house already. Paul is made up. She talks about trying to come to visit. I say something about going back across to see them when the baby comes. When the call is finished, I sit on the sofa and make tight fists with my hands, over and over. My skin is dry, and my fingertips rasp in my palm. My nails drag. Rough, rough noise. Bang, bang, bang. A cold current rushes over me and I'm up on my feet, out of the house, running out towards George.

I find her in the yard.

What's wrong? she says.

Nothing, I say, I just... I thought I could hear that noise again.

In the shed? she says.

I nod.

There's nowt in there for you to worry about, Ash, she says. You know what the wind's like here. Whatever you heard could be something right over the other side of the valley.

Shouldn't we check? I say. Make sure the girls are ok?

I'll check, says George. I don't want you in there, all worked up. You'll make them stressed and it's bad for the milk.

George is not a person you ask questions of. But that night, I force myself to ask how the butter and the cheese are coming. It's been months now that we've been milking, that she's been fermenting the butter and culturing the cheese, and there's nothing she's happy to sell, nothing she even wants me to taste.

Are things ok? I say. We're laid in bed side by side, not touching. I mean, out there, in the dairy? Is there nothing ready to try yet?

She's quiet for a while. Then she says, It's got to be right before it goes out. You only get one chance. You know how this business is.

We've been sampling outlandish things that George orders from other farm shops: cultured butters made with seaweed and miso and rose petals; raw cheeses crammed with garlic and nettles; stinking rounds of cheese made by

Trappist monks and silent orders of nuns. We're going to be simple, George has decided, but distinctively sour. Our butter will be raw—she skims the cream from the milk, to get rid of any sweetness, then mixes it with a culture and leaves it to ferment. What's left is muddled in a large, steel churn and then she hand-kneads it, salting to taste. The cheese will be raw, too. She's working on a signature cheese-custard, yellow as Irish butter but gluey and bitter. The hard cheeses she presses and wraps in cloth, storing them on the dairy shelves to ripen.

I can't get it right, she says. The butter is too pale. It must be because the girls are inside. I should have frozen more milk at the end of the summer. The hard cheese keeps cracking. And the custard keeps spotting with mould.

Can I help? I say. I could do more in the dairy?

No, she says quickly. No, no need, Ash. I knew it would be a long process. It's just trial and error.

In spring, things that vanished in the winter start to reappear on the moor: harebells, skylarks, the albino stag that the locals say has lived on the moor for an impossibly long time. George tells me she caught a glimpse of him in the pine woods, like a wisp of smoke through the trees. And other things appear, too, things abandoned or lost: a porcelain sink dumped in the middle of the causeway; a desperate fox nosing for food for her new cubs; a lad out in just T-shirt and jeans, cast up from the night before, walking the perimeter of our fields, off his head. *Am I in Halifax?* he keeps shouting. *I need to get to Halifax.* George circles him, keeping her distance, then makes him sit in a trailer and drives him down to the valley-bottom.

What is a boggart meant to be? I ask George one blustery morning. We're out in the field, patching up a wall that's lost a line of stones.

A boggart? she says.

I pass her a triangular rock and she jimmies it into place with her big, dextrous hands.

Well, it depends who you talk to, she says. Old Peter will tell you a boggart lives on a farm and helps when it's happy and hinders when it isn't. Makes mischief. Throws things around, bangs things, sits on your chest in the night. A right little farmyard poltergeist. She laughs. Ashleigh, she says. Don't tell me you're going soft.

Just trying to get to know the place, I say.

Well, she says. In folklore round here, the story goes that you can't escape a boggart. Once it's fastened onto you, it'll never leave you. In the old tales of Sour Hall, the farmer sets off to go, tormented by the boggart, but he finds the creature in his butter churn halfway across the moor. He knows then that he can't escape it, so he goes back to the farm, and learns to live with it.

Is that right? I say.

When I look up, George is staring at the barn. She's still smiling, but her face is straining against the wind. George has this look sometimes, like she's fighting something you can't see, and she's winning.

In April it rains for two weeks solid. It rains until the grates in the valley-bottom fill and the roads begin to surge with water. Then the Calder floods and the valley-bottom turns into a wide, brown river. Up on the moor-top, every surface gushes. The fields are spongy and give way under our feet, starting to turn to bog. It's twilight all day long, the rain stopping the light from breaking through. The lads can't get up to us, so I help George with the evening milking again. The cows stay inside all day now. It feels warm and damp and malarial in the shed. We herd them into place, line them up against the back wall, and fasten them up to the milking clusters. I lean against Vera, shoulder to shoulder. Her belly's big and hard now. She's due next month. She turns her massive head towards me, snuzzling my open hand with her wet, pale mouth as she's milked. She lurches suddenly, knocking me hard. All of the cows clatter, their hooves scrabbling around. Bang, bang. That noise, that noise is louder than I've ever heard it. The cows drag against the clusters. They bray and whinny like horses.

Whoa, steady girls, George calls. She walks down the line, checking them over. They're lowing still, big heads down, nosing for danger. You okay, Ash?

Yeah, I think so, I say.

Don't know what gets into them sometimes, George says.

Didn't you hear it? I say. The banging?

I heard the girls banging about, George says.

No, I say. It was in the dairy.

Maybe it's foxes again, says George. I'll check on it.

Don't— I start to say, but George's already through the doorway at the end of the shed.

It's nothing, she shouts. I hear her clattering about in there. Then she comes back through, wiping her hands on her overalls. It was just that old butter churn rolling across the floor, she says. Must've swollen in the damp.

George doesn't meet my eye. She pats Vera, who's still stamping her front hooves. There, girl, there, she says.

We work our way along the line, uncoupling the clusters,

leading the cows back to the pens. One of them half drags me across the shed, sprinting back towards the herd. When I lead Vera back across, she turns and blinks at me with whiskery eyes. She shakes her head from side to side.

Ash, George calls, stop mooning at the girls. I'll finish up. Go and have a hot bath and a big glass of wine. I'll be in in a minute.

The water here takes a long time to draw from the spring. I strip and I sit in the first few inches in the bath, waiting for it to fill around me. I try not to look at my body. When it's deep enough, I close my eyes and sink backwards until the water fills my ears. Everything is echoey and distant like this, but close at the same time. The muffled sound of my heart beating, the churn of the blood in my ears. Boof, boof, boof. What is that noise? My heart? The banging again? I open my eyes.

There are great blooms of rusty-orange spreading through the water. Bright streaks of blood and gritty trails of matter.

I'm bleeding. I must be bleeding again.

I hear myself scream. I'm screaming so loudly that I've killed the other noise and all there is is this scream, my scream, ringing in my ears and my throat.

George is in here then, and she pulls me out of the bath and wraps me in towels. She peers into the bath behind me and then she checks my body over, firm and careful, and she cradles me, just like before, rocking me again, holding me close to her.

Afterwards, she pours us both a whisky. We sit near the fire.

Ashleigh, she says. It's ok. You don't need to be embarrassed.

It wasn't blood in the bath. It was iron.

I screamed at the sight of iron.

She tells me now, by the fire, that the moors are studded with old mines. That when it rains like this, the mine shafts flood and the Sour Hall spring gets inundated with rusty water. With brown iron that makes the water taste of blood.

I should have warned you, she says. Didn't think to. I'd almost forgotten about it myself.

She's careful with me all evening—fixes me something to eat and more drinks. When we go to bed, she holds me close. And when the light's off, she says: Maybe you should talk to someone, Ash. You know, if you're still thinking about it.

I don't need to talk to anyone, I say. I'm not still thinking about it.

Alright, she says.

Once George has gone quiet, I don't think about it. I don't think about it really hard. There's a weight on my chest, or in my chest—as though I've swallowed water and my lungs are heavy with it. I remember a girl who used to work with us in the pub, a young girl, with purple hair and blue eyes and big, creamy cheeks, who used to complain about her boyfriend, about how gentle he was, how he didn't know how to take control, how it was pointless asking him to be rough—if you had to ask for it, it never felt real, did it?

I didn't answer her.

Is it my heartbeat? Is that all it is? This bang, banging. I put my hand across my mouth, bite down on the flesh of my palm. Bang, bang, bang.

It's May. The light has come back into the sky and the air is green and the cows are outside again. George says that the cheese is almost ready, that we're about to start making some money. She's cheerful. She tells me that it's Vera's time too. Vera's been pacing. The weight of the calf is low in her belly. Her udders are engorged and the soft ligaments under her tail have loosened, making a new spill of vulval flesh.

We take her up to the shed, put her in a side pen, and she lows and thrashes her tail around as though agitated by flies. When she has a contraction her body becomes something else: her tail shoots up in the air, her back arches like a cat's. She's silent and rigid then.

Is she ok? I ask George.

Vera's body is back to normal, cow-like again, but she's moving from side to side, and she's turned steadfastly away from us.

Yeah, says George, she's fine. They don't always like company in birth.

The labour is not quick. When Vera finally drops to her knees, the calf starts to show, like an obscenely large, glossy egg, pulsing at the centre of Vera's swollen vulva. It moves out, and then back in again, out and back in again. Finally, the calf starts to slide out. At least I think it's a calf, the creature's hidden in this bluish, opaque sac. Can't tell which part has come first, until the whole thing slithers out, and then I can see the front legs stretched in front, followed by the head and body. There is a small daub of blood left behind under Vera's tail, but something contracts, and the blood disappears back inside her. There's a vivid smell of fresh-cut grass and blood and milk. Vera's back up on her feet almost immediately. She sniffs at her calf. It's still; entirely still inside its caul.

It should be moving, George says. She climbs into the pen and pulls at the sac, which breaks easily. The calf moves its head ever so slightly and Vera begins to lick him, vigorously, all over. The calf's nostrils flare and then it barks, a hacking, old-man cough.

George moves off, back out of the pen.

The placenta was covering its mouth, I think, she says. Look at that. Our very first calf, clearing its lungs.

The calf lies there for a while longer, coughing, eyes only half open. Vera turns away from it to eat the afterbirth, then comes back to her calf and licks its face roughly. She licks and licks with her big, pale tongue until the calf is pushing back, struggling to stand up. Its back legs straighten first, and then it's on its front knees for a while, face grinding into the hay, until it finally judders up—thin legs splayed, body an unstable trapezoid. It's shaking and it jumps uncontrollably when it tries to move, but it's up and it's darting under Vera, stabbing its snout towards milk.

Well, says George, that is one of the quickest calves I've seen to feed. What a little beauty. And a bull calf, look.

I do look. I watch the calf feeding until my chest is tight, and then I turn away.

That night, the wind is high. There's been a gale warning. The slates lift on the roof of the house, and I think of hair being pulled up at the root. George is already asleep when I feel the weight on my chest again. A heaviness that is also a tightness. I don't think of it. I will not think of it. It was hardly alive at all. What use is there in thinking of it? Of the darkness, of the muffled sounds it might have heard? I think instead of a pub I used to work at in Liverpool that had a flat roof over the bar area, and a staff room that looked out onto the flat roof. I'd sit there in my breaks, reading the news, watching things on my phone, looking out at the sky and the plastic bags and crisp packets and parking tickets that got blown up on that roof and caught in the guttering. There were seagulls that nested over the pub and they made a great racket all through the summer, yawping at the dawn like a colony of seals. One summer a chick appeared on the flat roof. A large, grey seagull chick. Lifeless. Established dead by our team of bar staff who took up a rotating vigil in our breaks. No one knew what had happened to it, how it had come to be there, whether it had fallen from the nest, whether it had been suffocated by a plastic bag or poisoned by one of the objects that we sometimes saw the birds carry to their chicks—milk-carton tops and ring pulls and the slices of lime discarded from customers' drinks. When the mother bird discovered the chick, her cries were pitiful. At first, she stamped around the roof, cawing. Enraged; belligerent. She did this for several days. And then she sat down quietly, which was worse. She did not leave until the bar manager got out onto the roof through the hatch, bagged the chick up and disposed of it in the large wheelie-bin.

Bang. That weight on my chest, pressing down on me. Bang, bang. Something's banging out there again, banging in the wind. What a night for Vera and her calf, their first night together. Our first veal calf.

Is this really what kindness is? To let her lick the blood from her young, to let her smell and feed him, to let her believe in his life for weeks, for months, and then to take him to slaughter? Better, perhaps, never to have seen your young live. Better the old-fashioned way, the bullet in the calf's head. Bang. Bang.

Animals at Night

The cows are braying. The wind lifts the slates again, and then they clatter back into place. I should go and check on the shed in case we've left something unsecured. George has been working so hard. She needs her rest. And if I wake here, she'll only say I'm imagining things, or that the sound is from far away, dropped down the chimney breast by the wind. I leave her sleeping.

Out on the moor-top, the wind is wild and warm. I can smell earth and straw and the bodies of the animals. I'm wearing George's jacket and there's a torch in the pocket, which I use to light my way. Detritus swirls across the yard. When I reach the shed, there's no sign of anything left undone. The door is fastened properly. I open it, step inside, close it carefully behind me. Some of the cows are lying down. Some of them are standing together, heads jostling, big eyes reflecting oil-green in the torch's beam. Vera is standing diagonally in her pen. She's blocked the calf into the back corner and she's swaying from side to side. I reach my hand out towards her, but she doesn't respond.

Bang. Bang. Her hooves skitter, the whole herd skitters. They're all up on their feet now. Low mooing. Vera brays, head low, stamping her front foot.

They can hear it too. They can definitely hear it. The bang was from the back of the shed. The bang was from the dairy.

The door handle is cold to the touch. The air, as I step through into the dairy, is cool. A cold current rushes through me, makes my skin prickle. I flick the light switch and then the space is bright white. The smell in here is different now—sharp and yeasty. Curds of milk and rennet and something right bitter. The vats must be full of cheese. Fermenting. Ageing. There are large muslin cloths on the side, crusted with milk skim. On the floor, in a corner of the room, is the old butter churn. On its side. Knocked over in the wind, perhaps, though it looks so heavy, so sturdy. Bang, bang. Something banging in there, or in my chest? I take a step towards it. What would it be like to spend your life trapped inside something? This is what I used to think about, over and over, after it had happened. Bang, bang. There's something in the butter churn. There's something inside that butter churn. I had a baby once, or the start of one. It did not live. Or, it lived inside me and then it died inside me. It spent its whole life in the dark. It bled out of me the week I met George. It was kicked out of life. He kicked it out of life when I said I was leaving and then he set my hair alight. Bang. Bang. There's something in the butter churn. When George rang the doctors, they asked me to bring it in. Can you bring the matter in? they asked. The matter. Whatever is the matter? George scraped what she could from the bathtub, put it in the only thing we had to hand—an old margarine tub. A margarine tub, for pity's sake. Bang, bang, bang. My hands are on the butter churn. The wood is cool and tacky to the touch. My chest is tight, so tight. But I'm going to do it. I'm going to see what that banging is. I stoop to look into the barrel.

Nothing. There's nothing in here. Just empty space, the wood inside black and waxy too.

I stand up. That cold current in here—the east wind must have blown the butter churn over. I *am* going soft. The banging I can hear now, that thudding in the background, is the hooves of the cows next door. Is my own heart. Is the blood in my own ears. I right the barrel and shift it back against the wall, making sure it's on even ground. I put both hands on the barrel edge, breathe out. Ready myself to face the wind again.

And that is when I see it.

I glance back down into the darkness of the barrel and see it there. Its unmistakably foetal shape. Its clot of a face. Its small, curled, hairy body. That is when my body floods with the cold, and I cannot scream, because my throat is filled with something cool and sour and dense, and I turn and I run, I run through the stalls, back out into the darkness. I run and I run, and I've dropped the torch on the concrete, and the wind is a roar around me, bang, bang, banging in the amniotic black.

I leave a note for George. I have a small bag always ready, still. I know how to perform a flit. I set off when the pale, dawn light seeps up from the horizon. The wind has dropped, leaving behind a dead quiet. There is no bird song. Sheep cower silently on the ground. A whitish mist rises over the pine woods on the other side of the valley. I walk and I walk, and all I can hear is my breathing and my feet against the road. It takes me an hour to reach the bottom of the valley and the edge of town. I will catch a train. I will catch a train back to Manchester and disappear into some new work. I always do. George doesn't need me—I needed her, but she's never needed me.

I stand on the platform with my headphones in. I stand on the platform trying not to think. I press my fingernails into the flesh of my palms one by one, over and over. A train is coming, a train is coming, a train is coming along the tracks. The noise fills my ears like blood churning. Like butter churning. Bang. Bang, bang. I can hardly breathe, my lungs so heavy, my chest so tight. Bang, bang. Why is it still here? Why can I hear it still, even here?

I turn away from the train. I turn to try to escape the noise again and that's when I see her. George. Standing at the gate to the platform, her face blanched, her hands loose by her sides.

We sit in the greasy spoon in the station. She orders coffee, but neither of us drink it. I'm silent for a while and she doesn't ask any questions. But then I tell her everything. I tell her about the banging and the butter churn and the boggart. I tell her that I've always known how to get on with things, how to work and work to ward the bad things away. But I do not know how to get on with this—with Vera licking her calf into life and George taking care of me and the bang, bang, banging that makes everything come rushing back in, all of the sourest things—that kicking I got and the bloody scraps of life that me and George collected up together.

George stays quiet for a long time. Then she says: This is all I know, Ash. If you try to run away, it stays with you. You can't escape it like that. Come back with me. If you still want to be with me, then come back to Sour Hall and we'll see to this together.

The next summer, the sky over the farm is a haze of brightness; the hills are drenched with gold. The moor-tops have grown thick with purple grass and hare's tail cotton. George is making sour, delicious things, and she's selling them, selling them well—her fermented butters and custards and casein and hard, rancid cheeses. Vera's calf has grown to a yearling, a mad creature who charges the matriarchs. He'll soon go to stud.

I go out there often now. On the short summer nights when I cannot sleep, when I feel my chest start to tighten, when I hear the bang, bang, banging, I go out to the shed. The moon is a frayed thing in the summer sky. I walk through the warm, animal space of the stalls. I walk into the dairy and I sit next to the old butter churn. I feed it with memories of violence, and I coo to it, and sometimes, when the banging has finally died down, I put my lips to the cool, tacky wood, and I tell it that I saw it. Yes, I saw you, and George saw you too. We've both seen you, and we know what it's like to live in darkness and in fear. You were there with me at your very beginning. And you'll be there with me until the end. You bloody, fragile clot. You bright little scrap of life.

Acknowledgements

I am immensely grateful for the encouragement that came from friends and teachers who read my messy early attempts at short fiction—especially Abi Curtis, Dean Firth, Dulcie Few, Ted Few, Kate Murray-Browne and Nicholas Royle—all of whom helped me to stick at it. Thank you to the following for their invaluable feedback on work in progress: Camilla Bostock, Kieran Devaney, Michael Fake, Thomas Houlton, Laura Joyce and Helen Jukes. Thank you, as ever, to everyone at Dead Ink, and especially to Ella Chappell, for being the most patient and careful of copy editors, and Luke Bird for the brilliant cover design. Thank you to my wonderful agent, Sabhbh Curran, for helping to bring this collection into existence, and to Michael and Betty, for being my bedrock.

Earlier versions of some of these stories have previously been published as follows: 'Cluster' was published in *Best British Short Stories 2019*, edited by Nicholas Royle (Manchester), and appeared online as part of the longlist for the Galley Beggars Short Story Prize; 'Plausible objects' was published as part of the online *Quick Fictions* series, edited by Nicholas Royle (Sussex); 'Tell me what you like,' began life as 'Localised Quicksand' and was published in *An Invite to Eternity: Tales of Disrupted Nature*, edited by Gary

Budden and Marian Womack; 'Clean work' was published in *Test Signal: A Northern Anthology of New Writing*, edited by Nathan Connolly; 'Sour Hall' was commissioned as part of the Audible Original/Virago anthology *Hag*. I'm grateful to all of the editors for their input and for allowing this work to be developed and republished.

The line, 'One of the difficulties of establishing whether there's life on other planets is that there's no agreed definition of life,' was inspired by my reading of Daisy Hildyard's brilliant book *The Second Body*. My line, 'A shoal of mackerel—their bodies so exquisitely sensitive that a thousand fish move towards the deep as one,' was inspired by the research of marine biologist and oceanographer Sylvia Earle.

About the Author

Naomi Booth is the author of *The Lost Art of Sinking*, *Sealed*, *Exit Management* and *Animals at Night*. She is the recipient of a Saboteur Award for Best Novella and was named a *Guardian* Fresh Voice in 2019. Her short fiction has been longlisted for the *Sunday Times* EFG Short Story Award, the Galley Beggars Short Story Prize and anthologised in *Best British Short Stories*. Her story, 'Sour Hall', was adapted into an Audible Originals drama series. Naomi grew up in West Yorkshire and now lives in York.

Other titles by Naomi Booth

Exit Management

"At minus eighteen degrees, even the densest blood materials start to turn: the beginnings of a human heart will still into black ice."

Callum has been given an opportunity: József's house is the perfect place to live – plenty of room, a sought-after London location and filled with priceless works of art. All that József asks in return is for some company while he's ill and the promise that if it all gets too much, someone will be there to help him at the end.

It's fortunate then, when Callum meets Lauren who works in Human Resources and specialises in getting rid of people. József welcomes them both inside, and so begins a deadly spiral of violence. Pushed ever onwards by the poison of ambition, and haunted by loses from the past, these characters are drawn together in a catastrophe of endings.

Sealed

"We came out here to begin again. We came out here for the clear air and a fresh start. No one said to us: beware of fresh starts. No one said to us: God knows what will begin."

Heavily pregnant Alice and her partner Pete are done with the city. Above all, Alice is haunted by the rumours of the skin-sealing epidemic starting to infect the urban population. Surely their new remote mountain house will offer safety, a place to forget the nightmares and start their little family... but the mountains and their people hold a different kind of danger. With their relationship under intolerable pressure, violence erupts and Alice is faced with the unthinkable as she fights to protect her unborn child.

Timely and suspenseful, *Sealed* is a gripping modern fable on motherhood, a terrifying portrait of ordinary people under threat from their own bodies and from the world around them.

The Lost Art of Sinking

"You feel like you're falling into a dream."

They call it the Fainting Game and for the girls of Class 2B it's all the rage.

Esther is obsessed with passing out. Living in the Pennines with her father, Esther is willing to try anything in the pursuit of her rush. From snorting Daz powder to auto asphyxiation, the perfect swoon remains tantalisingly out of reach – so what happens when you take it too far?

Beautifully written, *The Lost Art of Sinking* is a haunting novella from one of the UK's most talented contemporary writers.